Until
SET ME FREE

An Until You Novel

Book One

D.M. DAVIS

Playlist

Say Hey (I Love You) by Michael Franti & Spearhead

Little Things by One Direction

Birthday Cake by Rhianna

Let me Love You by DJ Snake (featuring Justin Bieber)

Birthday Sex by Jeremiah

Then There's You by Charlie Puth

I Get to Love You by Ruelle

Kindly Calm Me Down by Meghan Trainor

I Miss you by Adele

Mercy by Sean Mendes

This Town by Niall Horan

She Will Be Loved by Maroon 5

For my husband, who believed in me from the beginning, and did *not* laugh when I said I wanted to write a book. He simply believed, as if it was the most natural thing in the world for me to want to do.

Kisses.

Until You
SET ME FREE

PART 1
GIVING THANKS
NOVEMBER

One

Samantha

OUTSIDE MY CHEM CLASS WINDOW THE SKY IS Caribbean blue with tranquil clouds. An easy breeze makes the leaves rustle like waving hands to the passing cars. The sun is high in the sky, shining like a hot summer day rather than the chilly fall day it is. I'd prefer to be out there than in here. It's the last day of school before Thanksgiving break, everyone is distracted and impatient for the day to end. Yet, I'm distracted and anxious for a whole other reason. My brother, Jace, is coming home to Dallas from the University of Texas at Austin—with his roommate, Joe.

What's Joe McIntyre like? Will he be approachable and talkative, or stuffy and terse? Will he treat me as an equal or as a kid? I know what he looks like. Anyone with a television, computer, or smart phone knows what the McIntyre brothers—heirs to the multi-billion-dollar technology company, McIntyre Corporate Industries—look like. They come from corporate-billionaire-handsome-rugged-GQ type sturdy stock. And the youngest of the three is coming home to stay for the week-long break.

"What are you going to say? Are you nervous?" A soft whisper and tap to my shoulder draws my attention.

Margot has known me since second grade and should know the answer to that is *hell yes, I'm nervous.*

"I'll probably just stumble all over myself either verbally or

1

physically." Being awkward with the guys in my school is bad enough, but god, I'll die if I actually trip in front of Joe.

Great. Now, I've probably just jinxed myself.

"I don't understand it, Sam. You're the smartest person at this school." She wags her finger, imploring me with her light brown eyes to accept what she's saying.

I roll my eyes. She's just as smart as me. We're both in the running for valedictorian of our senior class when we graduate in May.

Ignoring my obvious protest of her pep talk, she continues. "You're also smoking hot."

"Shh." I scowl, glancing around the classroom in case anyone overheard.

"Seriously? You think they don't know you're smart and beautiful?" She laughs. "You're a lost cause, Sam. Truly. How are you so shy and insecure when you have a brother like Jace—who's also crazy hot and smart, by the way. Y'all are gifted. I mean, jeez, you come from doctors and lawyers. There's not a bad gene in your family tree."

I can't help but laugh. "Margot, stop. You're working yourself into one of your rants. I appreciate it. I do. But I don't need you to try to build me up before I meet Joe McIntyre. I know who he is. I know who he will be. He won't give me the time of day."

I turn back around to face the front of the classroom. "I'm seventeen, for god's sake. What would he want with me when every college girl on campus is probably throwing herself at his feet?" I murmur more to myself than her.

After school, I rush through the door, excited to see Jace. Dropping my bag on the stairs, I move toward the baritone voice coming from the kitchen.

"Jace?" I holler.

"Is that my favorite sister I hear?"

"It's your only sister, jackass."

"Jackass?" His smiling face greets me at the entryway. "Is that any way to greet your favorite brother?"

I leap into his arms. "You're my only brother, Jace."

He stumbles back from the force of my lunge, stopping us from toppling over. His arms wrap around me, swinging me around, laughing at my exuberance.

I shut my eyes, trying to still the ache of loneliness. It's been too many months. "I missed you," I whisper.

He sets me down, his blue eyes piercing mine. "Missed you, too."

The kindness in his voice steals the tears from my eyes.

"Hey, no crying."

I nod and wipe my damp cheeks, sniffling. *God, I've missed him.*

He hugs me again. "We have a whole week together." His words hold promises I hope he can keep.

Releasing me, his hands remain on my shoulders as he searches for signs of more of my "girly emotions," as he calls them.

Satisfied the waterworks have stopped, he puts his arm around my shoulder and turns me to face the island where, lo and behold, sits the most beautiful man I have ever seen. My breath catches as I take in his dark hair, chiseled features, and skin that glows with sexiness. Or maybe I just had an aneurysm. That must be it. It's affecting my vision, because I swear he's glowing like a beacon. And my body responds as if he's calling me home.

What. The. Hell?

"Sam, this is my roommate Joe," Jace introduces the god in front of me.

How could I have missed him sitting there?

The beautiful man rises from his seat, his eyes glued to me. My gaze continues to rise as he comes to his full height. He has to be six and a half feet of solid muscle. His faded blue jeans and white t-shirt, tucked in at the waist, only accentuate his ripped torso visible under the thin fabric.

Holy mother of god, I can't breathe.

He moves closer, towering over me, his emerald-green eyes flickering across my face. "Samantha, it's lovely to meet you."

Lovely? Did this gorgeous hunk of man-cake just say it's lovely to meet me? Is he from the seventeenth century? I'm thrown off balance; my thoughts, my body, are in a whirlwind of sensory overload.

Somehow, I manage to take his outstretched hand. "It's Sam, and it's *lovely* to meet you, as well."

His slight grin spreads into a full smile with, *oh dear god*, dimples. They're not oh-aren't-they-cute dimples. Oh no, these are I've-got-a-dirty-secret-and-I-just-might-whisper-it-in-your-ear-as-I-fuck-you-senseless dimples.

He slowly lifts my hand to his mouth and kisses it. His sultry lips linger before he lowers our joined hands, still not releasing me.

The warmth of his touch sends shivers up my arm and down my body.

Danger is all I can think as my body screams *yes, please.*

"No one as beautiful as you should ever be called Sam, Samantha," he says seriously with just a bite of condescension.

I don't quite know what to think. He gives me a great compliment, calling me beautiful, yet makes me feel childish for loving my boyish nickname. I think it's sassy and free of pretension.

"Well, *Joseph*, perhaps you should get to know me before you decide my name doesn't fit."

He drops my hand, humor gone, but his eyes still hold mine. "No."

"No?"

He nods. "No. I don't need to know you better."

Wow. "Alrighty then." I turn to Jace, giving him a some-nice-guy-you-brought-home look. I guess Joseph's going for stuffy and terse and treating me like a kid instead of an equal. That's a shame.

Jace laughs, bumping me with his shoulder. "Joe, man, ease up. She's only seventeen. Sam suits her just fine."

"Nearly eighteen," I remind him, my chin rising in defiance.

He laughs again. "More like seventeen going on thirty-five."

He says it like it's a bad thing. I can't help it if I'm an old soul.

Joseph's still focused on me, sizing me up, I suppose. His face is unreadable, void of any emotion as he takes his seat back at the counter. I'm disappointed—I don't measure up. Then again, I already knew I wouldn't, so I shouldn't be surprised. If past experience drives future expectations, then I already knew I could never measure up to the likes of Joseph McIntyre.

"What are you doing tonight?" Jace draws my attention as he takes a seat next to Joseph. "Got a hot date?"

I scoff. "No. I'm working."

He knows better than to ask. As much as I notice boys, they rarely notice me. There was one, once. For a brief moment in time, someone noticed me, but I don't even try anymore. I throw myself into my studies, working on my AP college level classes that will allow me to graduate high school with an Associate's Degree in a mere six months.

"When do you get off?"

"Late. Eleven." I still feel Joseph's eyes on me, and it takes all I have not to glance his way and give him the satisfaction of knowing he's the reason my heart is pounding as my scattered thoughts ping around like a pinball machine. I wouldn't be surprised if my eyes gloss over and an out-of-order sign pops out of the top of my head.

I need to disappear for a while. Regroup. Take a cold shower. Run a marathon. Get laid. *Like that's gonna happen.*

Jace's face scrunches up, not liking my answer. He's overprotective, thinking I work too hard. He'd rather I was a carefree teenager instead of focusing on my future all the time. I don't work because I have to financially; I work because I want to. I need the experience. By nature, I'm an introvert. I prefer small gatherings, one-on-one interaction, to groups or parties. For my career aspirations in the corporate world, I need to be able to converse and interact with all types of people. I can't hide at my desk and hope someone notices my work. Technology is my passion, and the industry moves at the speed of light. I want to be at the head of the pack.

"What about tomorrow night?" Jace counters.

"I can't. I've got a term paper I need to work on."

He blows out a punch of air. "Sam, seriously, it's Saturday night. The weekend. You don't need to try to graduate college at the same time I do. You can be a kid, you know. You don't always have to be the most responsible person in the room."

"Says the boy who's in his junior year of college after only two years," I retort.

"Yeah, but I didn't start bustin' my ass until after high school." He motions to his roommate. "Joe, help me out here."

Joseph takes us in, running his hand through his wavy black hair, messing it up in that I-just-got-outta-bed kinda way.

I want to touch it, tame it.

"Come out with us, then you can work on your term paper on Sunday. Your brother just got home. He missed you. Spend time with him before you bury your nose in homework."

I didn't expect that. I thought Joseph didn't want to get to know me better, much less want to hang out with me. I can't focus on that dangerous territory. I don't have time for romance or a shattered heart, and Joseph McIntyre is an unrequited love-fest. He would eat me up and spit me out without a second glance, not because he's cruel, but because he's on a different level and wouldn't even notice the ant he just crushed as he walked by. *I'm the ant, by the way.*

Ignoring the angst in my stomach stirred up by Joseph's comment, I focus on Jace. "You really missed me?" He said it earlier, but only after I said it to him first, like an obligatory response.

Not missing a beat, he jumps up, making his way to me. "Don't start. You know I did." He squeezes my arm. "Come on. Come out with us tomorrow. I'd tell you to ditch work tonight, but I know you won't."

No, I won't ditch work. "What are y'all doin' tomorrow?" I shouldn't be considering this.

"We thought we'd go eat and then go to The Club, get our dance on, see who's home from college." He shrugs. "You know, see and be seen."

"I can't get in there. You know it's eighteen minimum age, and I don't have a fake ID."

He smiles. "I love that you don't. But Tommy's workin' the door and he already told me he'd get you in if you come with us. I promised him we'd only drink sodas. Plus, he's always had a thing for you, you know."

I grimace at the thought. "No. He's like...no." Tommy's like a brother, a silly, dopey brother. I nudge Jace, scowling. "You're just saying that. He does not have a thing for me."

Jace laughs. "He does—not that I'd let him touch you, but...well..." He shrugs, leaning against the counter. "It'll get you in. Come with us. Don't make me beg." He pulls out his big blue puppy-dog eyes.

"Are you gonna dump me to pick up women?" Jace is a manwhore, and has left me in the dust when I didn't have a backup plan to get home.

"Nope. Promise. Just you, me, and Joe here. No women. Though, you are a pretty good wingman," he teases me.

There were a few times I helped him seal the deal. I'm not proud of it. But honestly, if those girls don't know what they're getting into with Jace, I'm not going to be the one to break it to 'em. He's tall, dark, and handsome with those mischievous blue eyes woman fall for.

He's good to 'em. He just doesn't stick around for long.

He's young, sowing his oats, my dad says.

The apple didn't fall too far from the tree, according to my mom.

Apparently, my dad was the original manwhore until he met my mom. He says his heart didn't start beating until the day he laid eyes on his Eleanor.

They met at UT, in the quad. She was sitting under a tree studying, when my dad saved her from an errant football about to take off her head. He still lights up when he talks about that day, like she was sitting there and a ray of light shone down from Heaven leading him to her.

Mom tells it a little differently. Of the two of them, Dad is the romantic, fanciful one. And she's the down-to-earth realist.

They can't keep their eyes or hands off each other. I've come into a room more than a few times and had to turn around to keep from seeing more parental PDA than any kid should be subjected to.

I want that someday. I want a man to look at me the way my dad still looks at my mom. Like his life begins and ends with me. Like his next breath is tied to mine.

Someday. I hope. But for now, I can't live my life as a hermit, and I'll never meet anyone if I never go out.

"Is that a yes?" Jace asks.

"Yes, but I'm taking my own car. I don't trust you not to leave me in the lurch if you get a better offer."

Joseph laughs. "She knows you well, man." His eyes meet mine. "I won't leave you in the lurch, Samantha, but I'd appreciate the ride home if he dumps us both."

"Y'all suck," Jace growls, throwing his arms up and stomping out of the room.

He's not really mad, just sensitive about us not believing he won't leave us for a piece of ass.

Shrugging, I start to head out of the kitchen, but then feel bad for leaving Joseph. I turn around. "Do you need anything? Did Jace show you the guest room?"

"No, not yet. We came in the kitchen to eat as soon as we got in. I haven't even gotten my stuff out of the car."

When his eyes lock on mine, I swear I feel a zap of electricity running between us. His nostrils flare, and his chest rises. Am I affecting him as much as he is me? He looks at me as if he can read my thoughts, knows my desires, and can hear the quickening of my pulse.

He truly is a god of a man with his purely masculine features, thick wavy hair, and eyes that see things they probably shouldn't. He makes me feel things I know I shouldn't.

"Come on, Joseph, let me help you get settled."

His smile lights up his face and does crazy things to my body. "I'd like that, Samantha."

Two

Samantha

I MAKE IT TO WORK WITH PLENTY OF TIME TO SPARE. I didn't exactly sneak out of the house, but I did make a point to be quiet as I left my room and descended the stairs, hoping not to run into Joseph. He's on my mind enough as it is; I didn't need the added distraction of seeing him just before I left.

I love my job for two reasons. One: I don't have to focus on my future here. I don't have time to think about school work or what needs to get done for me to keep my high grade point average. This place is always busy, and I just have to focus on being friendly and making the few moments I interact with the customers as pleasant as possible. And two: I get to wear black. All black. Every day. All day. I feel comfortable in black. I feel safe. Secure. And even sexy. Sometimes.

"Hey, Sam." Trent, my friendly and on-spot boss, greets me as I put my purse away and clock in.

"Hey. How's it going tonight?" I'm sure he got here a few hours ago, even though he tries to keep his evening hours to a minimum for his family. That's a hard thing to do in the restaurant business when nights are where the money is.

"It's a good night. A bit slow for a Friday, but hopefully it'll pick up." He turns to leave. "Oh, there's a guy at the bar. He was asking for you."

My hand pauses midway to setting my time card back into its slot. "A guy? For me?" I hate the surprise in my voice. It's not likely a guy would be asking for me, but I don't have to make it so obvious.

He laughs. "Yes, Sam." His inflection is firm. "Take your time. Becca's got the hostess stand covered." He waves over his head as he slips out front.

As I near the bar, the air thickens and sizzles. And then I see him. Sitting there with his back to me, facing the door and the hostess stand.

Somehow, he senses me, turning as I approach.

That sizzle I felt a moment ago morphs into a full-fledged roaring inferno when his eyes lock on me. I stutter in my steps and trip into his side. He catches me in his capable arms as he pivots on his stool in one smooth, graceful move. Completely unlike me, who tripped over thin air simply because of the intensity of his gaze.

"You okay, Samantha?" He studies my face and rights my body, still holding me tightly around the waist against his solid chest, locked between his massive thighs.

Jesus. Fuck.

"I…uh…yeah." My hands splay across his perfectly-formed chest.

"Samantha?" His voice is low and powerful, like its pure frequency alone could produce enough energy to power a small town.

It's making my heart beat a million miles a minute and my brain foggy. "Hmmm?"

His smirking mouth knows too much. "You okay?" He clasps my cheek and encircles my waist, holding me securely in place. His green steamy gaze eats me up.

"Yes, I'm fine." I push away from the inferno that's Joseph McIntyre. "I'm sorry." I run my hands down my blouse and skirt like they need to be ironed out.

His hands release me slowly, as if reluctant to let me go. A chill courses through my body as the cool air hits the places he warmed with his touch.

If he notices, he doesn't let on. "No need to apologize. I'm just glad I was here to catch you." His eyes twinkle with mischief.

"I wouldn't have needed catching if you hadn't been here in the first place." I'm not clumsy by nature, but this man throws me off, keeps me off balance. Literally and figuratively. I knew I'd jinx myself worrying I'd trip in front of him.

He laughs. He actually laughs.

It's a nice round and robust sound. I can't hide my smile.

"What are you doing here anyway, Joseph?" I scan the bar. "Where's Jace?"

His smile drops. "He had a date."

I scoff. "Yeah, right. A *date*," I say with air quotes.

He shrugs, not confirming or denying. "My family's out of town," he says simply, as if that explains why he's here instead of at home or at a real bar hanging out with friends.

We stare at each other for a moment. It should be uncomfortable, but, strangely, it's not.

"I have to get to work."

"Have dinner with me," he says at the same time.

"What?" The word escapes before I can fully process what he said.

He looks chagrined. "Have dinner with me, Samantha."

I start to protest, but he raises his hand to halt my objection. "I know you're working." He motions around the restaurant. "They're not too busy. Perhaps they could spare you for an hour."

Ignoring my speeding pulse, I notice it might be possible, but really, it's just so unexpected. Why would he want to have dinner with me? I spot Trent watching us. He's amused, and I'm sure I'll hear about it later.

I step back. "I'm sorry. I can't." I make my way to the hostess station before Joseph can respond or change my mind.

Samantha

"Sir, I assure you we will seat you as soon as a table fitting your party's size becomes available." I shoot my co-hostess a look for assistance in reassuring this guy. He's offended we've seated others who arrived after his party and doesn't comprehend, or care, that the smaller parties he's referring to are easier to accommodate.

What group of eight men come to eat at the Cheesecake Factory, anyway? Go to a bar for god's sake.

Thankfully Becca smiles and assures him it shouldn't be much longer. I give her a nod of thanks.

"Well, honey, you're so sweet you make the wait worthwhile." He oozes with false charm, making my skin crawl.

"Thank you, sir." I reply half-hoping he was speaking to Becca.

He stays at the hostess stand, talking to his friends standing near the bar, but still within ear shot. "Pete, isn't she the sweetest? I think I should take her home."

Seriously? He's talking about taking me home like I have no say in the matter. I try to ignore him and scan the room, praying for a table to open.

"Yeah, man. Maybe she's got a friend or two who can join us," his friend replies.

I lean in to Becca and lower my voice. "Can you find Trent? Tell him we have a potential problem? If you don't find him, tell Bruce. He's big enough to scare them off."

Becca nods and flees. I wish I were the one leaving this uncomfortable situation instead of her.

"Where's your friend going, honey?" He doesn't seem to miss a thing.

I step to the side, keeping the hostess stand between us. He's making me uncomfortable, but it's nothing I haven't experienced. My customer service skills tell me to remain nice, until nice is no longer appropriate.

I've just about reached the tipping point. However, I'd rather Trent be the one to make that call.

"She's going to check the tables," I offer, trying to busy myself so perhaps he'll back off and give me a break. Unfortunately, they're the only group waiting at the moment.

He moves closer and grabs my arm before I can respond. He reeks of beer and cigarettes, making my stomach churn. "Why you hiding back there, honey? You should come out here and have a drink with us." His fingers dig into my skin as he pulls me from behind the hostess stand.

I gasp and try to jerk my arm free, but he's got a death grip on my upper arm. "Let go of me," I demand, working to steady my breathing and not give in to my rising panic.

He steps into me. "Not until you agree to have a drink with me."

"That's not going to happen." Joseph's deep voice comes from behind me. His arm wraps around my waist, and I instantly start to calm. "I suggest you do as the lady asks and release her arm." The menace in his voice cannot be missed by this guy, even if he's had one too many drinks.

"Find your own female. I saw her first," he spits back at Joseph, squeezing my arm tighter.

I whimper as his fingers dig into my flesh as he tries to pull me out of Joseph's hold. "You're hurting me." My voice trembles. *Shit.*

"I warned you." In a flash, Joseph has a death grip on the guy's wrist while he peels his fingers off my arm. I think if it weren't for my arm being attached to the guy, Joseph would have taken him down by now. But since I could be collateral damage, he's taking it easy until I'm free of his grasp.

Trent and Bruce show up with Scott, who's as big as a house and one of our head chefs. He puts his hand on Joseph's shoulder with a nod of solidarity.

Joseph releases the guy with a small shove, allowing Scott to step in.

Trent crosses his arms. "Sir, I'm going to have to ask you to leave the premises."

I'm not sure if it's Trent's words or the appearance of three more guys to defend me, but whatever it is, I'm thankful as the guy finally steps back. Joseph guides me back from the line of fire and into his side.

Trent, Bruce, and Scott step in front of us, forming a protective wall. His friends don't seem to want a fight, but the guy is not backing down and starts to make more of a scene.

Joseph walks us farther away before turning me to face him. "You okay?"

I nod. "He scared me. I'm fine."

I'm shaking. Why am I shaking?

He pulls me into his arms, and I don't resist. His hand cups my head to his chest as he holds me tightly. "You're okay, Samantha. I've got you."

I relax into him, feeling safe in the comfort of his arms.

With my eyes clamped closed, I'm lost in the feel of him holding me, soothing my body with his hands and gentle words. As I start to come down from the frenzy of whatever that was, my breath steadies, but I'm still off-kilter.

"You okay, Sam?" Trent asks from behind me.

Joseph pivots so I can see Trent without moving away from his embrace.

Trent's brow rises as he takes us in, making me self-conscious. I pull away. Joseph slowly releases me but captures my hand, keeping me close.

"Yeah. I'm fine." I nod toward the hostess stand. "Sorry about that."

Both Trent and Joseph snort in unison.

"You have nothing to apologize for. He's an ass," Trent says.

"I could have handled it better. Put an end to it sooner before he was even able to get close enough to grab me."

"Sam, stop. You handled the situation professionally and with class, which is more than I can say for him," Trent insists.

"He was trying to show off for his friends and too drunk to listen to reason, Samantha. Don't second-guess yourself." Joseph squeezes my hand.

Trent motions to Joseph. "If you're hungry, I can set ya'll up at the bar. Then take Sam home. She's had enough excitement for one night." He stops my protest. "I don't want to see you back here until the Friday after Thanksgiving."

"Trent, I have shifts on the new schedule. I can work. I don't need the time off."

"You won't be out any money if that's what you're worried about. You'll be paid for your shifts. But I think it's a good idea you take the week off. When you do come back, no walking to your car alone. Understand?"

"Yeah, I got it." I don't have it in me to fight. If he wants to pay me for not working, I'm not going to argue. At least not tonight.

"Good. It's settled. Order whatever you want; it's on the house."

He shakes hands with Joseph and gives me a quick hug before Joseph leads me to the bar. "Looks like you're having dinner with me after all."

I shake my head in mock disapproval. "Don't look so smug about it."

He throws his head back and laughs. "I can't help it. I like it when things go my way."

"Yes, I'm quite sure you do."

He looks at me pointedly with fire burning in his eyes. "Count on it, Samantha."

Three

Joseph

I'VE PRACTICALLY HAD A HARD-ON SINCE SHE walked into Jace's kitchen. Her sass, her confidence, and angelic face knock me clean over. And Christ, those blue eyes, long auburn hair, and red, pouty lips. She's Jace's sister, and she's only seventeen, but fuck me running backwards with a dog in my arms, she's something else.

Not like I'm thinking of her in that way.

Who am I kidding? I'm totally thinking of her in that way.

And don't get me started on loving how much she loves her brother. They have a great relationship. It's fun, but it's also genuine. They know each other and love each other anyway. Jace can't shut up about his kid sister. When my parents announced they were going skiing for Thanksgiving, I took the standing invite from Jace to spend the holiday with his family. I had no idea what I was in for. It probably would've been smarter to go with my brothers to Cabo. I can't say I regret it, though.

I can't get involved with Samantha. I know this. But as she worked the hostess stand in that fitted black skirt, simple black blouse, and nearly CFM black pumps, I can't seem to remember why. My mouth goes dry, my heart rate increases, and my thoughts go places they shouldn't. Not just because of my career priorities. Not just because she's Jace's sister. Not just because she's young, inexperienced, naïve, and has her whole future ahead of her.

It's all of those things that should make me run the other way as fast as I can. And yet, here I sit like a lonely sap, aching for a girl who looks like a goddess and is genuine to the bone. There is no pretense. What you see is what you get. If she's flustered, it shows. If she's mad, put off, it shows. If she's turned on, Christ Almighty, it shows.

Her fingers lazily skim the rim of her glass of iced tea. Her lower lip, captured between her teeth while her middle finger circles over and over again. It's sexy as hell, and my cock stirs at the sight.

Fuck.

"Are you sure you're okay?"

With a shy smile and minimalistic nod, she breaks the seduction of her iced tea, taking a deep drink.

Damn, if that's not sexy as hell too. *Double fuck.*

Maybe this wasn't such a great idea. Not dinner per se, but show-ing up at her work. Period. For the life of me, I don't regret sitting here in companionable silence. I don't give a shit if she doesn't say a word, I'm just glad she's okay after that man…I shake the thought away, lest I track him down in the parking lot. I can see her mind working, her face reacting in the smallest of ways to whatever's going on in that head of hers. I wish she would share. Particularly those thoughts that make her bite her lip and blush.

Christ. She takes my breath away.

"Tell me about your brothers. I know Fin is the oldest, and then Matt is your middle brother, but I don't know much else."

"Like you said, Fin is my oldest brother at twenty-five. He's great at his job, but he's an even better brother. He's single and looking, but he's more dedicated to the job than the search for *the one.*"

"Isn't he named after your grandfather? Finley McIntyre founded MCI with his brothers, right?"

More surprises from the auburn-haired beauty to my right. "Yes. That's correct." I turn to face her. "What else do you know about MCI?"

She swirls her straw in her drink, not meeting my gaze. "McIntyre Corporate Industries was founded by your dad's dad, Finley, and his brothers Maximus and Gabriel. Your father, Hugh, is the current CEO. Fin is the VP of Accounting and Finance, and Matt's the VP of Marketing." She glances sideways. "And you're going to be the VP of Product & Technology."

The last part, about me, was said with a pout, as if it makes her sad. "You've done your research."

She rotates on her barstool toward me, her lips drawn in contemplation. "I've met your brothers."

"Really?" Why didn't either of them mention having met Jace's sister? And more importantly, "Where?"

"They were really nice. Surprisingly down to earth."

My hand goes up. "Wait. Why do I feel like you're trying not to tell me something?"

Her crooked smile is endearing and draws me further into her spell. "Because I am."

I wait her out, arms crossed, one brow raised, with a smirk that trumps hers.

She breaks. Finally. "Okay…okay." Her blue eyes sparkle with mirth as her hands gesture in supplication. "Fine. I'll tell you. I'm actually surprised you don't already know. I interned at MCI this past summer—"

"What?"

"—I plan to return this summer and then apply for a job after college." She cringes like she's getting ready to give me some bad news. "And…apparently, you're going to be my boss."

Are you fucking kidding me? I've been groomed for the job by my father, grandfather, and uncles for as long as I can remember. I know everything about my department. I run my hand over my face and pin her with my stare. "Seriously? How did I not know this?"

"I don't know, really. Fin and Matt approached me last summer as I was leaving for the day. They introduced themselves, which was completely unnecessary. I was shocked they were approaching me." Her face lights up as she laughs. "I thought I did something wrong—that they were coming to fire or reprimand me."

"They never told me this."

"They said they'd heard Jace's sister was an intern and if I needed anything, to let them know. But…"

I lean closer. "But what?"

"I asked them not to treat me any differently. I want my abilities to stand on their own. I didn't—I don't—want any special treatment because of Jace." Her eyes sadden as her gaze roams my face. "Joseph, I didn't know you were Jace's roommate, not then. It was only a few weeks ago, when you decided to spend Thanksgiving with us that Jace told me his roommate Joe was…you. *Joseph McIntyre.*" She sighs in resignation. "Imagine my surprise."

"I don't have to imagine it. I'm feeling it right now, Sweetness."

"I'm really sorry. I don't expect anything from you. If it'll be a problem…I'll…" Her voice breaks, and she quickly glances away, but not before I notice her eyes welling up.

I can't see her tears, but her hands dash them away quickly.

Christ, this girl. "Samantha." I grip her shoulder. I can't let this upset her. She's had a hard day as it is. "We'll figure it out. It's not worth getting upset over." Not, now, anyway.

She nods, still not meeting my eyes. "I could go somewhere else," she says so softly I nearly miss it.

A surge of pride swells through me that my family's company means so much to her. "It means a lot to you, doesn't it? MCI?"

Unshed tears glisten in her eyes, yet there is a fire inside them that burns deeply. "MCI is on the cutting edge of technological advancements. It's all I've ever envisioned for myself. Everyone said I was too young to know what I really wanted, but I knew as soon as I saw that story about MCI developing a software program for the space shuttle—I had to be a part of a company like that."

"That was years ago." I think back. "I was only thirteen or so. Jeez, you would have been…ten?"

"Yep." She beams brightly.

Christ, she sounds like me. Discovering what she wants so young.

Just knowing, in your gut, when something was right, but more than that—actually pursuing it the way I've done. I stare at her, study her face, her shy smile and blush that creeps up her neck as I don't let up. "You're remarkable." I finally breathe out.

I'm not sure I actually said it out loud, until her blush deepens.

"No," she says incredulously. "I…" She shrugs on a sigh. "I just knew."

She doesn't have to say any more. I get it. I totally get it.

Our food is delivered, and we return to our companionable silence. My mind is anything but silent with racing thoughts about this unexpected woman beside me. I've never been a partier, even in high school. When most of my friends were out drinking and getting laid, I was focused on technology and the future of MCI. Now, I see the woman next to me is not any different than me: streamlined, proficient, voracious focus with little time or interest in typical teenage carousing ways.

Her hand lightly brushes my arm, and I glance up to see her eyeing me expectantly. Shit, I missed what she said. "I'm sorry, what?"

Her smile unforgivingly pulls at my heart. "I asked about Matt. Are you closer to him since he's only a few years older?"

"You'd think so, but, no. Fin and I are cut from the same cloth. Matt and I look alike, but Fin and I are twins on the inside. He calls me nearly every day, keeps me on the straight and narrow. He's my sounding board, friend, and mentor." I take a sip of water.

Understanding glows in her eyes. "That's nice. What's Matt like?"

"Matt is twenty-three. He's actually like Jace. Personable, well-liked. Entirely too popular with the ladies."

Her eyes light up as she laughs. "Ah, another manwhore?"

"I was trying to have more tact, but yes. He's incredibly intelligent, easily bored, needs new challenges. I've often wondered if that's the reason for his womanizing ways."

Mischievously, she leans over and bumps my shoulder. "Or, he just really likes the ladies."

I chuckle. "Or he really likes the ladies."

"How is it you'll go from being a college student to being a Vice

President? How does that work exactly? I mean, doesn't the current VP resent you swooping in and taking his job?"

"This has been in the works for a long time. I started training for the job when I was thirteen. Worked my way through the different departments, different jobs, different responsibilities. Once I decided on the technology wing of the business, my focus was…" I shrug, not wanting to come across a smug. "…razor sharp." I couldn't get enough, still can't.

"My Great Uncle Max, Maximus, will retire once I take over. I attend key meetings and keep up with the quarterly reports, meet with him weekly to stay abreast of what's going on. Plus, he'll remain as my mentor for a few years, before he fully retires." I pause for a drink. "He's looking forward to retirement, as is my Great Aunt Vi. She says he works too hard and is looking forward to traveling."

"Wow, it sounds like you're already working full-time for them."

I push my plate away. "Nearly. I don't have much time for anything other than school and work. It's been my single-minded focus for so long. I'm not sure I remember a time that it wasn't."

"That brings up an interesting point." Her blush is back, and her eyes evade mine.

"And what is that?"

She surprises me when her eyes boldly lock on mine. "Why are you here?"

I study her for the briefest of moments. "I don't really know, to be perfectly honest. I'm having a hard time staying away, even when I know I should."

She nods, breaking eye contact to scan the bar.

I'm not sure what that reaction means. "But I'm glad I was here." I touch her hand, squeezing lightly to bring her attention back to me. "I'm sure Trent and the other guys would have handled that asshole customer without my help." I duck my head to catch her eye. "But it makes me sick to my stomach thinking of you here, shaky and upset with no one to comfort you."

She leans against my arm. "I'm glad you were here too. Though, I feel like I wouldn't have been nearly as upset if you hadn't been here."

I scowl. "Why? I made it worse?"

"Not...worse. There's something about you, Joseph. It's like you make it okay for me to be vulnerable, instead of keeping it in. Because you were here, I was able to feel the weight of it by acknowledging it."

"You say it like it's a bad thing. You don't always have to be strong and stoic. It's okay to rely on others for support, comfort."

"I've just...never had that."

How can that be possible? She comes from a great family. Why does she feel she has to be an island unto herself?

"Why is that, Samantha?"

With a shrug of her shoulder, she looks away. "I guess I've always been rather self-reliant. People—my family—expect it of me now. It's become a given. They assume *Sam can take care of herself.*"

Christ. "Just because you can, doesn't mean you should."

"Maybe. Or maybe because I can—I should." Her eyes search mine as if seeking some sort of affirmation from me.

"I'll never agree to that. We all need support, especially from our family. Do you ever ask for help?"

She laughs, but there's no joy in the sound. It's a sad laugh that twists my heart. "No, Joseph. I don't. They have enough going on in their lives; they don't need any of my teenage drama."

"What about tonight? Will you tell them about that guy grabbing you?"

"No." She scowls at me. "And neither will you. It will only make them worry, needlessly."

"Samantha."

"No," she says more firmly, then picks up her tea and finishes it off as if it's the last of a desperately needed beer. "We should go."

What happened? I thought we were having a connecting moment, and now I feel relegated to the backseat of the car like a child. A child who needs to mind his own damn business.

We'll see.

PART 2
THE BLOOM

Four

Samantha

THE MORNING LIGHT STREAMS IN FROM THE GAP in my curtains, like laser beams cutting through the fog of sleep and igniting the memories of last night. It's not every day I get rescued from an asshole and have dinner with my hotter-than-sin rescuer, who in all likelihood will be my boss if I'm lucky enough to get a real job at MCI. Not to mention the fact that he's a future vice president and millionaire.

"For all I know, he's already a millionaire," I mutter to the floating dust particles dancing in the beam of light as if they too just woke up. They seem much more alert than me.

He held me in his arms. Joseph McIntyre not only rescued me, but then comforted me like he'd known me forever and it was his *place* to protect me. His right. I wish it were. I wish he could see me for the woman I hope to be and not this teenager who's more geek than beauty queen.

"God. Sam, get a grip," I mutter, rubbing my eyes. "He was just being nice. He'll never see you that way."

I roll to my side and flinch. "Ow." I forgot about my arm. I lie on my back and examine it. Finger-shaped bruises mar my skin. I guess I won't be going sleeveless tonight.

On a sigh, I sit up. Should I even go tonight? Maybe I could talk Margot into going with me. I could use a buffer between me and Joseph. Or rather, between me and my desire for Joseph.

I send her a quick text to call me when she wakes up and then head to the bathroom. I throw on some yoga pants and an oversized t-shirt, grab socks and shuffle to the kitchen for some much-needed caffeine.

With my mug and phone in hand, I slip out to the back patio and curl up on a lounger by the pool. The temperature is chilly but the morning sun and my coffee should keep me warm enough.

My black gold is half-gone and cooling off faster than I'd like when my phone rings with Margot's "Single Ladies" ringtone.

"Hey."

"Hi. I'm sorry I didn't call you sooner. I went for a run and just saw your text."

"You're crazy, girl. The sun's barely up, and you're out running."

"I like to run in the early mornings best. And why are you up? You like to sleep in on Saturdays."

"I don't know. I woke up early for some reason."

"I hear birds. Where are you?"

"I'm in the backyard by the pool, having coffee and talking to my friend Margot."

"Smarty-pants."

"I know, but you love me anyway," I tease.

"I do. To what do I owe this early morning phone call?"

"I wanted to see what you were doing tonight. Jace and Joseph want me to go out with them, and I was hoping you'd join us."

"Aww, I can't. The Dubois women are getting ready to leave for our day of pampering and evening of debauchery. Well, as debauched as it gets with my sister, Mom, and Grandmother." She laughs.

"So, you're going to a strip club then?" I snicker at the thought.

"You know it. I've been saving up my singles so I can shove them in the male stripper's g-string using only my mouth."

"Eww. That's a visual I'm not sure I can ever scour from my brain. Thanks for that."

"You're welcome, Sammykins."

I laugh at her silly nickname for me. "Have fun."

"You too. I want all the juicy details about tonight!"

"Uh, I doubt I'll have any details to share." Or none that I'm ready to admit to.

"We're still doing movie night sometime next week, right?"

"Yeah. Monday or Tuesday?"

"Monday would be better. We start cooking for Thanksgiving on Tuesday," she suggests.

"Okay, let's plan on it then."

"It's a date."

I head inside for a fresh cup of coffee and to start breakfast, but the smell of bacon wafts in the air. Someone beat me to it. Mmm, one of my favorite smells. I freeze at the doorway when I spot Joseph at the stove flipping pancakes and turning over bacon. *That's a beautiful sight.*

"Good morning, Sweetness." His voice is gruff from sleep.

"Good morning." I refill my cup. "Would you like some coffee?" I spot a mug on the counter. "Or a refill?"

"A refill would be great."

"Shouldn't we be cooking for you?" I refill his coffee and add sugar and cream to mine.

He glances at me and then returns his focus to the stove and the tasks at hand. "I figured it was the least I could do for crashing here all week. I could stay at my parents' house or Fin or Matt's, but I'd rather be here than alone at their places."

"I can understand that, but solitude is nice too, sometimes."

He places pancakes and bacon onto two plates and hands me one, his forehead creased as he pins me with his eyes. "I think you spend too much time alone."

I take both plates and move to the kitchen table. "I don't mind being alone. I'm not one of those people who can't stand the silence of their own thoughts. I rather enjoy my company."

Our coffees in hand, he joins me at the table, sitting across from me. "I rather enjoy your company too." He pushes the butter and syrup my way.

"I rather enjoy your company," I whisper back, afraid even that simple truth is too big of a confession.

"That's good, 'cause we're gonna see a lot of each other this week."

I grab the milk and two glasses, pouring him one without thinking. His disarming smile sends my heart racing as I hand him his milk. "How'd you know I wanted milk?"

I shrug. "Who doesn't want milk with pancakes? Or anything sweet for that matter."

"True."

The house is all too quiet for a Saturday morning. "Where is everyone?"

"Your parents went to the gym, but said to save them some food and they'll eat when they get back."

"When did they leave?"

"You were on the phone when they left."

"Oh. And Jace?"

"I haven't seen him, but his car's not out front, so I assume he didn't come home last night."

I nod as I dig into breakfast. "Thank you for this, by the way."

"You're welcome."

"I was talking to my friend Margot earlier, and she'd just come home from running. Now my parents are at the gym." I point to our food and back at him. "I feel like I need to go exercise after this."

He pauses mid-sip. His forehead furrowed, considering my statement. "I could go for a run."

His mischievous green eyes and smirk stop my chewing. "What?" I murmur around my bite of food.

"Wanna come with me?"

"Sure, why not."

Why not? I can think of a million reasons why not, but all of them escape me at the moment as my sense of daring clouds my better judgment.

Joseph

That evening, Jace and I visit with his parents while Samantha gets ready to go out. I've met Daniel and Eleanor a few times. Daniel is a successful plastic surgeon who specializes in reconstructive surgeries. He primarily focuses on birth defects and traumatic injuries. He has quite a large military clientele.

Eleanor specializes in corporate law. My dad has tried to lure her to come work for MCI for years, but she's happy in her current gig. She and my mom serve on several charities together. Our parents were friends before I met Jace at UT. Oddly enough, we don't hang out together as families. My mom swears we all met when we were just kids, but I truly don't remember. If I had met Samantha before, no matter my age, I would have remembered her. She's captivated me from the moment I set eyes on her, and after our dinner last night, she's burrowed her way into my thoughts and won't let up.

Samantha trots down the stairs, hotter than any seventeen-year-old should be. I thought nothing could be hotter than the shorts and tank top she wore for our run.

I was wrong.

She's a classic in black jeans, black heeled boots, and a black sweater that nearly hangs off her shoulders, accentuating her curves. She's the epitome of understated sexuality. To top it off, her auburn hair flows down her shoulders and back in sensuous waves.

If I didn't know better, I would think she's the older sibling instead of Jace. He has the same strength and confidence of character, but comes across more as a good-time Charlie, whereas Samantha has a fierceness burning inside her, dying to break out and blaze a trail across everything she encounters.

With her looks, personality, and most definitely her quiet strength, it's no surprise guys her age aren't chasing her. She's intimidating as hell. They wouldn't know what to do with her if they caught her. She's not someone to take lightly. Her waters run deep, and if you're not a powerful swimmer, you'll surely drown.

She needs a man who's not afraid to let her be the woman she's meant to be, to let her stretch her sizable wings, giving her space as she takes off, and then wait and watch her soar, praising her heights and accomplishments. She needs a champion, a guardian who will stoke those flames, give her strength when she needs it, and be her safe place to land.

I stand when she descends the last stair, her smile lighting up when she notices. She motions for me to sit down as she kisses her parents hello, and then makes her way to sit on the edge of the couch where I'm sitting. I take it as a compliment, her choosing to sit next to me instead of on the other couch with Jace. Pride swells. I want to beat my fists across my chest in display of my manhood, of my possession of her.

Christ, alpha much? Tamp it down. This is Jace's sister. She's seventeen. She's not ready for you.

Not now, but maybe someday, she will be.

"Hey," she whispers over her shoulder. The soft curve of her lips and the mischievous twinkle in her eyes make my cock stir.

Holy hell, not yet.

"Hey," I reply, nearly short of breath, my fingers twitching to touch her, pull her into my side, under my arm. Safe. Secure. Protected.

Five

Samantha

THE BEAT-BEAT-BEAT OF THE MUSIC THRUMS through the walls and floors and into my chest. A mash of wall-to-wall bodies sway and bob in continuous motion either to the music or to the bump and grind of those around them. The lighting is low and sensual, yet bright and exhilarating at the same time, constantly changing with strobe and spotlights in never-ending motion. There is no stillness, no solitude, no sanctuary from the constant assault of the senses.

It's fucking amazing!

"This way, Sweetness." Joseph's lips brush my ear as his warm hand envelops the curve of my waist, ushering me through the throng of people.

He glances down at me, and the flash in his eyes sets my pulse racing. We follow Jace to an upper level corded off with red velvet ropes. Joseph takes my hand and my elation blooms as he leads me up the stairs. His hold on me is firm, protective. There's something about his large hand engulfing mine that makes me feel safe with him.

Jace speaks to the large bouncers guarding the entry through the velvet ropes. After a moment, they shake hands with Jace and Joseph, waving us in, giving me a friendly nod as I follow. We're shown to a private sitting area with three couches set in a U-shape with end tables and a glass coffee table in the center. Jace selects one end of the center couch. Joseph sits next, pulling me to sit between them.

Only once I'm seated does he release my hand. I bring my new-ly-freed hand to my lap, touching it lightly to see if it feels as hot as it seems. My skin is enflamed from his simple, possessive touch.

I'm taken back to last night, him coming to my rescue, protecting me from the overly aggressive customer, then comforting me in his embrace, ensuring I was okay.

I was fascinated and entranced by his enthusiasm for being part of MCI. He talks about it like it's a Mom-and-Pop operation when it's one of the largest technology companies based in the United States, definitely the largest in the South.

I hope to return there after I graduate from UT, but having a crush on the future VP isn't going to do me any favors. I don't want any special treatment. I want my every achievement to be because I earned it, not because the heir apparent twice removed is my brother's roommate and friend.

...and apparently has the power to make my girly parts come alive.

"Sam." Jace's voice brings me back to the VIP lounge. He motions to the waitress. "What do you want to drink?"

"Oh uh, a Coke, please." I tune out again as they order their drinks.

The view from up here is even more spectacular. The entire club is five stories high, with each level open to the main atrium dance floor area below. People are hanging out over the ledges, peering down at the lower levels and those on the main dance floor. The vibrations are just as strong up here, but the music is not nearly as loud. It's actually possible to carry on a conversation.

Joseph bumps my leg with his. "Are you okay? You're awfully quiet."

I barely glance at him as I answer—I'm more focused on the ladies they've attracted who have taken up residence on the other two couches. "Yeah, I'm just taking it all in." I wonder if he'd be hitting on one of them if I wasn't here.

Get over yourself, Sam. He's going to pursue who he wants whether you're here or not.

Our drinks arrive, and Jace and Joseph continue talking over me.

Sometimes to me, but mostly to each other and the ladies vying for their attention. It's uncomfortable. I feel awkward and like the odd man out.

I lean forward and scan the room. How many hundreds of people are actually in here? I can't imagine how much money this place brings in each night. There is no single-women-get-in free discount, at least not on this hopping Saturday. Although, technically, we got in free, as Tommy let us slip in after tagging Jace and me as under twenty-one.

I want to get a closer look at the atrium and the other floors, but mostly, I want to escape feeling like the ugly duckling in a sea of swans. I stand up, barely making it to my feet before a hand captures mine. I know that hand. He's only touched me few times, but it's a touch I could never forget.

I peer down at Joseph questioningly.

"Where are you going, Samantha?" His voice is commanding, stirring things inside me I shouldn't be feeling for someone like him. I can't forget who he is. Who he will be. Despite last night's events and our remarkably relaxing dinner, I'm not the woman for him. Maybe one of these women are future VP wife material. But it's not me. He only represents heartache for me.

I motion to the ledge. "I just want to get a better look. This place is amazing." I glance from Joseph to Jace, whose focus doesn't shift from the woman nearly sitting on his lap. Veronica. *Shit.*

Joseph releases my hand. "Don't disappear on us." The concern on his face makes me think he really means "don't disappear on *me.*"

Stop. It. Now! Don't go there.

I force a smile. "I'm not going anywhere, Joseph." Except away from here…and *her.*

Skirting around the women, who've slowly crowded in closer, I move toward the ledge and grip the handrail for support.

It's no big deal. They're in their element. You're the one out of place.

"Let it go," I chastise myself as I scan the dance floor. It's an incredible effect seeing the entire floor vibrate with moving bodies in time with the music. It's choreographed chaos. I'm entranced, giving myself over to the rhythmic beat of the music and the swaying bodies. I close my eyes and tip my head back, taking a deep breath. I can feel his eyes on me, or I imagine they are. It doesn't matter, the effect is the same. I shiver. My skin pricks with goosebumps, and my nipples harden.

"Have you been here before?"

I'm pulled from my reverie by a voice to my right. It's one of the bouncers.

I shake my head. "No. It's incredible." I'm sure my face shows my awe. I hope it doesn't betray my inexperience.

"I didn't think so. I'd remember seeing you," he says sincerely.

I laugh out loud. "Right. In this sea of people, you'd remember me?"

He studies me intently, his eyes landing on my lips before returning to my eyes. "Yes, I most definitely would." He reaches out his hand. "I'm Paul."

"Sam." I shake his hand. "It's nice to meet you, Paul." I survey the club. "Is it always this packed?"

He laughs. "The night is still young. We're only at fifty percent capacity." He points up to the top levels. "See, there's hardly anyone up there. Give it a few hours and you won't be able to find yourself, it'll be so full."

I giggle at the notion. "I had better not lose myself then, huh?"

"Best not to, but if you do, just come find me, and I'll help you find yourself," he says with a teasing gleam in his eye.

Warmth covers my back and a strong arm wraps around my waist. Paul looks up into the face of whom I can only imagine is standing so close to me, blanketing my entire back. His scent fills the air around me, and his hard body presses into me. Joseph.

I tilt my head to meet his eyes, those green orbs that tell me so much, but instead I see a sternness in the set of his jaw and coolness in his eyes, not so much for me, but for Paul, I think. I'm not sure what that look means, not at first, but Paul backs away, nodding to Joseph, almost in supplication to his authority.

His authority over me?

"Do you do that often?" I look away, hiding my smirk and elation that he came after me.

"Do what, Sweetness?" His voice tickles my ear, his arm still firmly wrapped around my waist.

"Take ownership of things that don't belong to you?"

He chuckles in my ear, his chest rumbling against my back. "Perhaps I just took ownership of what needed to be taken."

Holy shit.

My heart races like a train getting ready to jump the tracks and pulses between my thighs. I need to get away from him. "I need to dance." I step out of his embrace.

"Not alone, you don't." He lets me move away, but only slightly, his hand resting on my hip to keep me close.

Behind him, the couches are now full of women glaring at me. "Where's Jace?" And Veronica?

"He spotted someone he knew." His tone is flat.

"You mean a *woman* he knew?" I don't know why I have to drill home the point.

"Yes." I see an apology on his lips.

"That took less time than usual." I shift, sweeping the club, wondering if I can spot him.

"He'll be back. He hasn't left you." His voice sounds so sure, as if he knows something he has no clue about.

My gaze slowly meets his. I want to touch his face, run my fingers through his hair and kiss those lying lips. "You sure about that?"

He moves closer, pressing against me. "No." The need to apologize for my brother is back on his face, but I know the score. When it comes to choosing hanging with me or getting a piece of ass, the ass wins every time.

I turn away from Joseph, not wanting him to see the thoughts I can't hide. "You don't have to babysit me," I say over my shoulder, not even sure he can hear me.

He moves in front of me, lifting my chin. "Samantha."

I close my eyes, jerking my head away. "Really. I can take care of myself. Go, have fun. Find your own woman. I'll see you before I leave."

Run.

I walk away, but only make it two steps before he captures my hand.

Joseph

"Not happening, Sweetness." I pull her back to me. "I'm no babysitter. I'm here because I want to be."

I don't let her avoid my eyes. I hate the pain I see there. She puts on a brave front, but it obviously hurts her when Jace dumps her to chase a girl. I bet Jace has no idea he crushes her spirit just a little each time he does it. Each time he shows her she's not a priority to him. She, on the other hand, is always there for him whenever he needs her. I hear him on the phone with her, texting her, emailing her. She's always there, quick to reply. Available to him, always.

I scan the room. Dancing is not my favorite thing. I prefer dancing in private, the horizontal kind of dancing, where you only need a partner and no spectators, and music is completely optional. But she likes to dance, and at the moment, I would do anything to lift the sadness from her eyes.

I wrap my arm around her. "Stay close." I head for the stairs.

She peeks up at me, her eyes wide. "Are we leaving already?"

Would she leave if I asked her to?

I stop in my tracks, running my thumb across her jaw, wanting more than anything to kiss those pouty lips. "No, beautiful, we're going to dance."

The smile taking over her face makes my heart jump.

"Really? You'll dance with me?"

I chuckle. "You might not call it dancing, but I'll try my best."

On her tip-toes, she wraps her arms around my neck, giving me a quick hug and a kiss on the cheek, scorching my skin. "Thank you."

"Don't thank me yet."

I let her lead us as we weave our way onto the dance floor, letting her decide where she wants to do this.

As she stops and turns toward me, someone bumps her from behind, shoving her forward into my chest. Instinctively, I wrap her in my arms, swinging her around so my back is to the offending person.

"I'm sorry." She breathes across my chest, her hands resting on each pec. A pink flush creeps up her cheeks.

"Don't be." I loosen my grip and move to the music. It's a fast song, but we sway slowly, in half time to the beat. She doesn't push away, and I'm in no hurry to relinquish her.

I want to hold her close, like I did last night after that asshole dared to touch her. It took everything I had not to rip the hand touching her from his body. But her boss and the other guys had it handled, and she needed comforting more than me acting like a caveman. And I needed to be reassured she was alright.

As the music morphs into a slow song, Samantha's bumped again, and this time I pull her flush against my body, my arms around her back protectively, in an effort to cocoon her from further threats.

"Did you just growl?" Her amusement twinkles in her eyes and in the curve of her need-to-be-kissed lips.

Shit. Did I?

"Possibly," I simply reply. Though there is nothing simple about how I feel about this woman. Before I'm ready to lose the feel of her in my arms and the warmth of her touch, the slow song ends, and we're back to the club mix. The positive note? I get a close-up view of her gorgeous body as she works it to the music, finding her own rhythm to each song. I try to keep up, hold my own, but truly I'm just along for the ride—and what a beautiful ride it is.

37

She gets lost in the music, her shyness forgotten, her body leading instead of her brain. Passionate. That's what she is when she dances. It's intoxicating to watch, but I don't want to just watch. I want to be a part of it. I want to be consumed by her fire. I want to burn with her.

Fuck. I've got to get a grip.

Two more songs, and I convince her to take a break. Back on the couch, catching our breath, the waitress is quick to hand us two bottles of water. I spot Jace on the far side of the dance floor, grinding with that girl from the couch.

"Do you know her?" I point in their direction.

Samantha follows my line of sight and quickly diverts her eyes when she sees them. "Yep. Not a fan."

Her fidgeting hands and the way she chews on her bottom lip hint that there's a story behind her dismissive tone.

"What'd she do to you?"

She inhales sharply, pinning me with her eyes. I've hit a sore spot, nailed the crux of the issue.

"Nothing worth talking about." She motions toward the stairs. "I'd like to go up to the top and check it out. Would you come or would you rather stay...and..." She glances to the women surrounding us on the couches. "...find another dance partner?"

Another dance partner? It's the second time she's insinuated I might prefer someone else's company to hers. "Why do you think I don't want to hang out with you?"

"I'm going up." She ignores my question, finishes her water, and walks over to the bouncer who spoke to her earlier.

He points to a particular staircase as he whispers in her ear, standing too close for my comfort. Samantha smiles at him and nods, glancing back at me as I join her before she exits the VIP area.

"What was that about?" I try to hide my irritation.

"Paul was pointing out the quickest way up to the top, but you need special access. He said he'd tell them we're coming." She stops her progress, glances over her shoulder. "Are you coming?"

Man, I'd love to. *Crass, man. Not cool.*

"Lead the way." I press my hand to the small of her back, needing the contact.

We have no problem gaining entry to the roped-off stairs; we're even given passes to the terrace lounge on the roof, which is more elite in its admittance. I try not to stare at her ass as we climb the stairs, but it's impossible when it's right in my face. The sway of her hips, the brush of her hair across her back, and her little glances back at me to be sure I'm still here captivate me.

The stairs are empty, so I could climb next to her. I don't for two reasons: one—she could have a misstep in her boots, and I'd rather be behind her to catch her, and two—why would I give up the best view in town?

We stop halfway to take in the expanse of the atrium and dance floor below. It really is a nice place, all four sides surrounded by the upper levels, looking out over the atrium and across the way to connecting platforms surrounding each level.

I glance at Samantha, but her attention is elsewhere. She's spotted Jace on the dance floor with that girl grinding against him. The pensive look is back.

"What happened, Sweetness?"

With a quick half-hearted smile, she dismisses my question again and moves away from the ledge, climbing up the stairs to the roof. Whatever it is, she obviously doesn't want to talk about it, but I'm not sure I can let it go that easily.

At the top, we give our passes to the gatekeeper, entering through the double doors, and still as the cool breeze hits us to take in the rooftop opulence. There's a glass surround along the entire edge. The seating is broken up into different areas, each resembling an outdoor living room with lush chairs and couches surrounding a fireplace. Some sitting areas accommodate large groups, while others are smaller, intimate and private. As a backdrop, there's a maze of trellises with greenery and lighting woven throughout.

I lead her to a more private area, situated away from everyone else. She moves closer to the glass, gazing out over the Dallas skyline. "It's beautiful."

"Yes, it is." Though I'm referring to the beautiful woman reflecting back at me. I'm lost in her. She doesn't notice my preoccupation. She has no idea what she does to me.

I wave off a waitress, not wanting to be disturbed.

"Tell me," I prompt again.

She shakes her head *no*, but her whole body stiffens.

I brush her cheek with the back of my hand. "Come sit by the fire and talk to me."

I'm relieved when she agrees, and I'm able to pull her to my side on the couch with my arm over the back, resting behind her, itching to touch her.

"What classes do you have this semester?" She tries to sidetrack the conversation, but I'm not letting this go. It obviously bothers her, and the fact that Jace has ditched Sam for this woman is concerning to me. I need the facts before I decide whether to mention it to him or not.

"Tell me."

Her big blue eyes shimmer in the firelight, piercing through any pretext I still harbor that I will not, one day, make this woman mine.

Mine. The thought resonates in my head like a bell.

"I'd really rather not talk about this, not with anyone, but especially not with you."

Her body is riddled with tension, her face is cautious, guarded. Her walls are up, and instead of letting it go and giving her respite, I want—no, need—to charge forward, knocking down any barrier between us. I can't explain it.

I don't normally have to try so hard, but mostly, I don't really care if they let me in or not. Sex has been the guiding force of all my relationships. I'm not interested in serious. I'm focused on the goal—graduating top of my class and sinking my teeth into MCI. It's not just a job. It's my future, my birthright, my focus. But this face, this woman, makes me want more.

More.

Everything.

I try not to balk too much. "Why not me? Do I seem disinterested, like I don't care?"

"No, that's not it." Her eyes cast down at her hands clasped in her lap.

Christ, I can feel her emotions burning her up inside. *Let me help, Sweetness.*

"Then why?" What's so wrong with me, for fuck's sake?

She sighs in exasperation. "Maybe because I don't want you to look at me like I'm a loser."

I lift her chin. I have to see her eyes to gauge her responses, her feelings. But mostly because I want to be seen by those remarkable soulful eyes. "That could never happen."

She laughs me off and tries to move away, but I still her with my arm around her shoulder.

"You don't know me well enough to say that, and you already made it quite clear you don't want to get to know me. Remember?"

What was last night, then? Why the fuck does she think I was there? For the cheesecake?

Christ, fuck. What are you doing, man? She's not ready for you.

She sighs. "My name."

"I should have cleared this up last night. I didn't make myself clear." I lay my hand over hers. I'd draw her onto my lap if I thought she'd let me. "I never meant that. I just meant, knowing you better wouldn't change my opinion about your nickname. I'll never believe *Sam* is suitable for someone such as you."

"*Such as me?* What does that mean?" Her brow furrows.

She has no idea of the storm she stirs in me. "It means, Samantha, I believe you are far too exquisite to go by a boyish name such as *Sam.* Your beauty requires a more suitable name." I squeeze her hand. "Maybe even Goddess. You're blushing. Have I embarrassed you?" I want to see how far her blush goes.

She meets my eyes. "How can you be so comfortable saying such things? You're older, sophisticated, good-looking, and well-bred. You're not supposed to notice a girl like me."

What the hell? She's from a good family. She's beautiful, exquisite even. How could I not notice her? "For the record, I don't agree. But, for now, I'll just say, I do notice you, and you are no girl. You might be three years younger than me, and perhaps more naïve in certain areas, but you are no young girl to be dismissed, not noticed, or not taken seriously."

She smiles at me genuinely. "Thank you, Joseph. That might be the nicest thing anyone has ever said about me."

Christ, I hope that's not true. This girl needs consoling from a heinous lack of compliments.

"Now, tell me what she did to you." *I'm not letting this go.*

She settles a little more under the crook of my arm. "She dismissed me. Negated my importance. She takes great pleasure in taking things away from me."

I still. That's not at all what I thought she'd say. "What's her name, anyway?" *If she's hurt you, I need her name.*

"Veronica Hamm. She's a year older than me. Honestly, I don't really even know her. I don't think I'd actually had a single conversation with her before she showed her distaste for me. She truly dislikes me, and I haven't a clue why."

"What did she do?" This Veronica is pissing me off. How could she not like this angel in front of me?

"The first time I met her, she was hanging on Jace's arm, glued to his side. She's a *clinger.*"

"A clinger?"

"Yeah. Girls who latch on to a guy, all fake, all boobs, no brains or pretend to have no brains, feeding the guy's ego, and lashing out at any perceived competition." She stares at me. "I imagine you've known a fair number yourself."

I laugh. "Yes, maybe a few." I know exactly the type she means, and I don't stand for it. If a girl shows her claws, her cattiness for no apparent reason, she's gone. Jealousy is one thing, but being purposely mean and snotty is another.

"She didn't like me talking to Jace or the fact he stepped away from her the minute I said I needed to talk to him. She got all rude and in my face afterwards. When he wasn't around, of course. In front of him, she's all fake smiles and pretense. It didn't matter to her that I'm his sister. Time was time, and she wanted all of his."

"I can't believe Jace would put up with that." I've seen him dump girls for less, and I can't believe he would ever put up with anyone being mean to his sister.

"As I said, he didn't know."

"You didn't tell him?" For fuck's sake.

She cocks an eyebrow like I'm an idiot. "I'm the kid sister of Jace, the pussy whisperer. You think Veronica is the first, last, or only bitch to give me shit?"

"Such language." I try not to laugh at her spirited delivery of a very sad fact.

"I'm sorry. It's frustrating." She sighs. "I love him. I'd do anything for him, but sometimes the reality of the bimbos he tends to go for is just too much to put up with. I mean, Jesus, will he ever grow up, grow a pair, and have a real relationship with a grown woman who doesn't think a blowjob is synonymous with a handshake?"

"Wow, that's a pretty apt description of Jace's type." Sad to say, it's spot on.

She's gone quiet, staring at me, studying me, it feels like.

Does she see me? Does she see the man—or does she see what my future can do for her?

She's not like that.

"Is that your type too?" she whispers, almost apologetically, like she doesn't mean to offend me if that's the case.

"Fuck, no." I scowl. "Listen, I don't disagree with anything you've said. But just because we're friends doesn't mean I roll the same way he does. Jace is a sprinter. I'm more of a marathoner, in it for the long haul."

Well, once I find the one I want. And, Sweetness, I want that girl to be you.

She nods, seemingly accepting and relieved by my answer, which I find quite satisfying. "Explain to me how this Veronica is different from the way all the other *clingers* treat you."

She pauses, contemplating. I can actually see the moment she gives in to me. The moment she lowers her wall, just a fraction, to let me peer over.

That's right. Let me in, baby.

"There was this guy, Roger. We went out. Dated. Hung out at school, had lunches together, talked in the halls. Everyone knew we were kind of an item, new, but still, something was there. It wasn't a secret, or just in my head. He openly pursued me in school and out."

A secret?

What's going on with the dumbfucks in her life? She's elated from my compliments and has to point out that a guy actually liked her in public and didn't keep his attraction for her a secret.

She shifts on the couch. I sense her discomfort, and I imagine it's because of what she's going to say next.

I pull her closer to me. "I've got you," I say softly. "It's just a memory, but I'm here to help any way I can." Thankfully, she relaxes into my side.

"One of his friends stopped me before last period telling me Roger wanted to meet after school by the football field." She looks up through her lashes. "I thought it was kinda sweet, like a secret rendezvous."

Jealousy rips through me. Though I can't be with her right now, I sure as fuck don't want anyone else to have her. Not even a taste.

Mine.

"When I got there, I couldn't find him, not right away. It was off-season for football so there were only a few people milling around." She squirms again in her seat, leaning forward this time, putting distance between us. "I found him eventually. Well, I found *them*, under the bleachers, of all places. Such a cliché. Veronica was on her knees, giving him a blowjob. I just stood there, shocked, unable to move. But, then it got rougher. He was pumping into her. Hard. Holding her head in place with his hands. She was gagging…choking." Her voice cracks with emotion.

I place my hand on her back, needing to touch her. She glances over her shoulder long enough for me to see shame mixed with unshed tears in her eyes.

I want to break Roger and Veronica for hurting her like this.

"I've never…I didn't know…" She stumbles over her words. "I was actually afraid for her. I moved closer. Despite who she was. Despite who he was, and what they were doing together, I feared for her safety. I thought he was hurting her. Until I heard him say *'Take it deep. Show me what Sam will never give me. Fuck, that's right, all the way, babe.'*" She cringes, shuddering from the memory.

Christ, the idea of talking to Samantha about taking it deep would've turned me on under any other circumstances, would have made me *hard*. But not this. The idea of these two getting it on in front of Samantha, contaminating her with their vile act while talking about *Samantha* taking it deep or not, actually turns my stomach and flips my protective instincts into high gear.

She stands up and moves to the edge, placing her forehead against the glass. "This is humiliating. Why would you ever want to know this?" she says so softly, I never would have heard her if I hadn't followed her.

Like I could have stayed away.

Mine.

I place my hands on her shoulders, squeezing slightly. She's trembling, and my chest hurts for her.

"He's a fucking idiot, and she's a royal bitch." I kiss the top of her head. "This betrayal is not about you. I mean, it's not a reflection on you. You have no reason to be humiliated, embarrassed."

She wraps her arms around herself. "I call bullshit on that." She takes a staggered breath. "Anyway, she must have heard me, saw my movement or something, as her eyes locked on mine, and the vitriol in them almost knocked me over. Her hands gripped him, and whatever she did with her mouth pleased him greatly by the sounds coming out of him.

"It hit me then. She did it on purpose. She wanted me to see, to find them, to put me in my place, to take him from me. Though, he obviously wasn't mine to begin with." She sighs, shaking her head. "It took another second, but I finally turned and walked away. I'd only made it a step or two when she called, '*Where you goin', Sam? You're gonna miss the best part.*' Then I heard Roger's voice, '*Goddammit. Fuck. Sam! Get off me, you bitch. You did this on purpose. Sam, wait!*'"

"I didn't look back. I didn't stop. I just kept walking."

Six

Samantha

WE NEVER DID SEE JACE WHEN WE LEFT THE CLUB shortly after my rooftop confession, my humiliation laid bare for Joseph to witness.

Why did I share that? And with him of all people?

The humiliation.

The rejection.

The shame.

He looks at me as if he really sees me. It's unnerving and exciting, all at the same time.

But nothing can come of it.

I can never be his.

It's probably all in my head, anyway. He doesn't really see me. Am I so desperate to be seen that I'm projecting my desires onto him? Joseph McIntyre would never want a girl like me. Not for a night, much less forever.

Not me.

Joseph drives my car home. I feel shaky and too lost in my memories to drive, and he kindly offered. He's just being nice, watching out for Jace's kid sister.

As soon as we get home, I head to the stairs, Joseph hot on my trail, only a few steps behind me. I grab the banister, pausing before taking the first step. His footfalls stop. I don't look back, but I can feel his nearness.

"Thanks for tonight. I…uh…I'm tired. G'night," I force out in a rush and bound up the stairs as quickly as I can.

Hide.

"Samantha." His voice is closer than it should be, he must have taken the stairs two at a time.

Shit. I freeze at the top of the stairs. "Yes?"

The steps creak as he moves to stand directly behind me. I close my eyes, my heart pounding in anticipation of his touch, but it doesn't come, not in the way I expect. I thought he might grip my shoulder or arm. Instead, his whole body presses against my back, his warm breath skirting my neck.

I glance back only to come face to face with his lips. *Fuck, those lips.* He's a step below me, still taller than me, but his lips are dangerously close in proximity to mine.

He brushes my hair off my shoulder, sweeping it to the other side. His fingers graze my skin and make me shiver. "Are you okay, Sweetness?"

No. Hell, no. Please kiss me. Make me forget Veronica and Jace, and that damn embarrassing story I told you.

"Yes," I chirp, my voice way too high.

His fingers trace the curve of my neck. My breath catches and automatically my head tilts, giving him better access.

"Why is it I don't believe that's true?" His words trail down the same path as his fingers, and my knees nearly buckle.

Jesus, I have to get out of here before I make a complete fool of myself.

I step forward, immediately missing his warmth. I turn, nearly facing him, unable to make eye contact. "Other than dying of embarrassment, I'm just fine." I dare a selfish glance, aching to see his face. I need to see the truth of this moment.

He ascends the last of the stairs and stops right in front of me. "Don't." His deep voice resonates between my thighs. "Don't give them that power over you."

Yes, he's right.

I simply nod and slip away down the hall.

"Samantha."

His plea doesn't slow me down. I keep going. Shutting my bedroom door behind me. Shutting him out. Shutting out the possibility of what would have happened if I had stayed in the hall until things progressed. How long would it have taken for him to walk away? Instead of finding out, I walked away first.

I strip as soon as my door clicks closed and head for the bathroom, turning on the shower. Feeling undone from Joseph and covered in the memories of Veronica and Roger, I need the comfort of the hot spray on my body.

I wash every inch of me. Twice. Even my hair, despite having just washed it a few hours ago.

By the time I get out, dressed, and dry my hair, it's late, after one. I should go to bed, but I'm keyed-up, revitalized by the shower.

I head to the kitchen for a drink of water and a snack.

Finishing my last strawberry, I hear a sound behind me. I turn.

Standing in front of me is the sexiest man alive, in just a pair of black workout pants that sit low on his hips. His upper body is even more cut than I'd imagined, and of course he has an eight pack, because a six pack would be too common. He's tan with the perfect amount of hair on his chest and abdomen.

His happy trail.

Jesus.

He's the perfect male specimen.

If I were a painter, a sculptor, he would be my muse, my model.

If I were a composer, I would write a symphony about him.

If I were more experienced, I would drop my panties and beg him to take me places I'm convinced only he can take me.

My eyes travel up his body, taking longer than they should. When I finally reach his face, his jaw is clenched, his eyes are burning hot, and his chest rises and falls with each breath. He seems pissed.

Why's he pissed?

"Hi," I say softly. My voice, my face, my body betray my lecherous thoughts, I'm sure.

He silently stalks closer, giving me the same perusal I just gave him.

It'd be funny, if it wasn't so sexy. My heart pounds faster with every passing second.

His eyes latch onto my breasts, and it's only then I realize what I'm wearing, or the lack of what I'm wearing: black boy shorts undies and a white cotton camisole. No bra. And to top it off, I can feel how hard my nipples are, which grow painfully harder from the realization he's seeing me in my underwear.

"Shit." I fold my arms over my chest, clutching my forearms.

Some sort of animalistic sound emanates from his chest as he steps closer, looking as if he wants to devour me.

Devour. Me.

"Too late, Sweetness." His voice betrays him as well. He licks his lips. "I've already seen those delectable nipples."

Shit. Shit. Shit.

I squeeze my thighs together and tighten the grip on my arms, trying to contain the rage of lust he's released throughout my body.

He moves closer, placing his hand on my hip. "I'm going to kiss you." He scans my face, landing on my eyes. "If you don't want me to, you need to tell me now."

Shit.

I don't respond. I can't even keep his gaze, much less form any words.

He unfolds my arms, his eyes locking on to the handprint-shaped bruise around my arm. "Son of a bitch," he hisses. His fingers gently explore the marks. "Does it hurt?"

The concern in his voice is enough to unhinge me. The lump in my throat prohibits my answer.

He bends down and brushes his lips across the bruise. Slowly. Reverently.

It's such a tender gesture that seizes my breath and sends a torrent of chills through my body. "Joseph," I whisper.

He rises to his full height, cupping my cheek. "I want to kill him for hurting you, Samantha." His other hand continues to caress the bruise. "He marred you. He hurt you. He manhandled you." He's getting worked up, and not in a good way.

"I'm okay. You were there to save me. You protected me. You stood up for me." I choke on the last part. No one's ever stood up for me.

His eyes flash, catching on to the gravity of my words. "I would never let anyone hurt you. Ever."

My head spins from the words coming out of his mouth, the tenderness of his touch, and the desire on his face. *How will I ever survive you, Joseph McIntyre?*

I don't say anything. I just nod.

He runs his thumb across my lips. "I'm going to kiss you."

My breath hitches again. I picture those same lips that were just grazing my arm doing the same to my lips.

"Samantha?"

I'm stunned. I can't move. I can't even think.

His thumb traces my lips again. "If you don't want me to kiss you, you need to tell me."

Isn't my non-answer telling him what he needs to know?

His head moves closer, his lips grazing my cheek, then his nose nuzzles my ear. "Cat got your tongue, beautiful?"

Jesus.

The shudder his voice and warm breath produce has me wet and weak in the knees. There's no way he didn't feel my body quake.

I nod.

He smirks, humor and lust dancing in his eyes. "Well, at least your head works. Let's try this. If you don't want me to kiss you, shake your head *no*."

I nod my head *yes*.

His emerald eyes stare into mine; his thumb continues to caress my bottom lip. "Is that a *yes* you understand, or a *yes* to kissing you?"

I think I'm going to die if he draws this out any longer. "Jesus. Fuck. Kiss me already."

He growls.

This time I heard it for sure. He fucking growled.

"Such language," he whispers against my lips. "I've tried to resist you, this pull between us. I…it's stronger than I am."

"Joseph," I warn.

"Impatient much?" he teases me. "Anticipation, Sweetness."

"I think if I have to endure a second longer, I'll explode." I start to back off.

He grunts his disapproval and pulls me flush against him, closer than before, securing me with an arm around my back. "We can't have that." His lips brush across mine, and then his tongue runs the seam of my lips. "Fuck me, you taste like strawberries."

"Such language," I chide.

"Give me those lips."

There is no more teasing, no more anticipation, just raw desire. His warmth, his taste, his need overwhelms me because it matches mine.

His hand holds the back of my neck as his lips move slowly, tenderly, arousing every inch of me to his touch. The clean spicy scent of him and the remains of his cologne engulf me. The hand on my back moves lower over my ass. He squeezes and then pulls me closer still.

I gasp as his erection pushes against me. His tongue slips past my parted lips, slaking his desire, consuming my mouth.

My hands move in opposite directions, one to his ass and the other into his hair. I've been dying to touch his silky black mane, and his tresses do not disappoint. He moans as my fingers grip his hair, ensuring our kiss does not end too soon.

His hands slowly lower to the back of my thighs, lifting me, placing my legs around his waist. The kitchen counter is cool against my ass as he sets me down, like a fresh breath against my heated skin. He settles between my thighs, his embrace pulling me flush against him, pelvis to pelvis, chest to chest.

"Better," he breathes across my lips. I pull him back to my mouth; he doesn't resist, but he does chuckle. "My greedy girl."

"More," I whisper before his lips return to their rightful place—against mine—in a deep soulful kiss.

His growl reverberates through my chest before it reaches my ears. My nipples ache, wishing his hands, his lips would search them out. No man has ever touched my breasts, much less kissed or sucked them. I moan at the thought, which only spurs him on, kissing me feverishly.

As if he can read my mind, his hands relinquish their current positions and take residence along my waist, moving slowly up to the bottom swell of my breasts. I arch toward him. His hands squeeze lightly.

Touch me, take me, make me yours!

When his thumbs finally graze my nipples, I whimper from the immediate pleasure that shoots between my thighs. I want more. No. I *need* more.

He does it again, and again. Gently at first, and then lightly pinching and pulling, making me crazy with lust, with need, with things I don't even have the words to express.

His.

He pulls away, his breathing heavy. His needful eyes scan my face as his thumbs continue their teasing. "Has anyone ever touched these beauties before?"

As soon as I answer. This. Will. End.

If I affirm my innocence, he will feel guilty for touching me.

If I say he is not the first, he will feel guilty for continuing my corruption.

I lose either way. I lose him, no matter what I say.

"Sweetness?" he prompts as he kisses the corners of my mouth.

"I don't want you to stop." Jeez, I sound desperate.

On an exhale, his head lowers to my shoulder. His warm breath tickles my neck as he draws air in and out of his lungs in long, stuttered breaths.

His hands still.

My head falls forward to rest against his shoulder, and I close my eyes. A tear skates down my cheek. "Please don't regret kissing me," I murmur into his bare skin. My heart's heavy at the idea of him regretting touching me.

I knew it was too much to hope for.

I know better.

I'm a fool.

His head rises, and his warm hands capture either side of my head, lifting my face to his. His thumbs swipe my tears away before his lips press to each makeup-free eyelid and then down my cheeks, following the tears' trails.

His lips brush mine before he pulls away. "The only thing I regret is our circumstances, our timing. If we were both in a different place in our lives, I would not hesitate to make you mine, in every way."

His.

I smile and nod, liking that.

I take comfort in knowing he feels the same pull for me, and for now, that's enough.

Maybe someday it can be more.

I can only hope.

"Come on, let me walk you to your room. It's late and I need to get my beauty sleep." He grins.

Holding my hand, he laces our fingers together as we silently walk up the stairs to my bedroom.

At my door, I face him. He leans in, and softly presses his mouth to mine and then whispers, "Someday, Sweetness."

He steps back, our hands still joined, fingertips to fingertips, barely holding on, not wanting to let go. That wisp of a smile is back on his lips. "So, answer me now. Was I the first to touch them?" He nods at my breasts.

"Would it make you happy if I said *yes?*" The dimpled smile that spreads across his face is answer enough. "Yes," I whisper.

He nods, understanding what that means to both of us. He slowly moves away, forcing our hands to part. "Goodnight, beautiful."

I wrap my arms around myself to keep from reaching out to him as he backs down the hall. "G'night, Joseph."

I watch as he makes it to the end, his eyes meeting mine before he enters his room. With a final nod, we back into our respective rooms and close our doors.

Seven

Joseph

WISH I COULD SAY I HAD A RESTFUL NIGHT. IT started out that way. Peaceful, full of promise of a future with the amazing creature just down the hall from me.

But then my thoughts turned back to earlier in the evening. Jace abandoning her. The treatment she endured from his passing hook-ups, and lastly the horrific vision of Samantha coming upon Roger and Veronica. I could still see the shame on her face when she imparted the details to me, and to think, Jace was probably with that witch as I lay there steaming.

I did eventually fall asleep, but it was fitful at best. I wake in the morning in time to greet Samantha and her parents as they make their way out the door. My gaze lingers on Samantha, as does hers on me, before the door closes.

Someday there will be no more doors between us.

I make my way to the kitchen to feast on the food Eleanor promised was warming in the oven. I text Jace and tell him to get his ass home, pronto.

An hour-and-a-half later, he finally graces me with his presence.

"Jace, you dumbshit, I've got a few things to talk to you about." I motion to the fridge. "You'd better get us a couple of beers; you're gonna need it." I don't care that he's underage at the moment. We're in his parents' house, and we're not going anywhere.

He joins me on the couch, handing me an open beer. "What'd I do now? Is this about last night?"

"You're a fucking asshole for leaving your sister last night, especially when you made a point of saying you wouldn't, and even got all pissy when neither of us believed you. But the reason I'm pissed off is larger than last night."

I take a long draught of my beer and rest it on my knee, trying to retain control of my rage. "You're gonna have to forgive me. I've had all night and part of the morning to get all worked up over this. This is probably going to blindside you, but there are things you need to know. Things you need to take control of. Fix."

"Jesus, Joe, what the fuck's going on?" He glares at me as he takes a drink of his beer, waiting.

"Did you at one time tell someone, or get the word out, about your sister being off-limits?"

His eyes flash with guilt.

I guessed right.

I sigh and roll my eyes. "What the fuck did you do, man?"

His hand snakes around the back of his neck, rubbing it, embarrassed. "There was this asshole a few years ago. I don't even remember his name. I caught wind about him talking about Sam. Me and a few friends cornered him one night and confronted him. He confirmed what he and his friends were saying and thinking about Sam."

His blue eyes glisten with sadness, making me think of Samantha's last night. "She was fourteen, Joe." He stands and starts pacing. "It kills me to think of what they were saying about her. Fucking fourteen! Barely out of playing with dolls and shit, and these guys were talking about getting balls deep in her. Fuck!" With a sigh, he faces me. "And that was the nice shit they said. Anyway, I beat the crap out of him and told him to pass it along to his friends that Sam is off-limits, then, now, forever. My buddies did the same." He sits down, finishing off his beer.

"I understand why you did it, and I'm not sure I would have handled it any differently, but maybe you should have told her. Not what they said about her, but about you putting the fear of God in them, that she was hands-off."

"Why's this coming up now?" His voice is solemn, calm, but still on edge.

"She thinks she's a leper or something. No guys talk to her, or hit on her, and if some guy does show her any attention, she's so shocked, she eats it up like it's her last fucking meal. You meant well, Jace, but she needs to know she's not undesirable. She's fucking beautiful and doesn't deserve to be alone because you and your friends put a ban on her."

"You think my sister is beautiful?" His protectiveness comes on full-force again.

I sigh. "Man, I think she's more than that. I think she fucking hung the moon, and it breaks my heart she doesn't see it. And before you get all in my shit, I know she's seventeen. I'm not going to conquer her, if that's what you're worried about. But I do see her, and what I see is amazing. I can envision a future with her, when we're both older, more mature, out of college. But not now. I can't give her what she needs now. I can't be the one to help her see how incredible she is.

"She needs you, Jace. She needs her older brother to let her spread her wings and dip in the dating pool before she becomes an old spinster because she shut herself off from everyone, thinking she wasn't worth anyone's time or effort."

His eyes widen in shock. "She really thinks that?"

Dipshit. "Jace, her own brother dumps her for another woman at every turn. You're showing her how guys are supposed to treat women. Your pump 'em and dump 'em mentality is setting the precedent for what she can expect from men in her life. She called you the pussy whisperer and said that you only date, and I'm using the term *date* very loosely, women who don't know the difference between a blow job and a handshake." He flinches. "Is that how you want guys to see your sister?"

"Fuck, no." He runs his hand down his face.

"Well, then maybe you need to man up and stop chasing every

woman who's an easy lay. Plus, you need to tell Samantha about the injunction you put on her. She needs to stop thinking there's something wrong with her."

I actually really hate saying that. I don't want her to date anyone. Anyone other than me, that is.

"Okay. I'll talk to her." He gets up, taking our empty beer bottles, and comes back with fresh ones. "Anything else?"

"Yep, there's two more things."

"Two? Fuck me. I think I'm gonna need some tequila."

I laugh. "Nope, there's no way I'm letting you get shit-faced. It's bad enough I'm sitting here drinking beer with you. But honestly, I need it after the last twelve hours."

"The fact that you, man of steel, are upset, is not making this any easier. If it's got you riled, then it's gotta be bad."

"It is. I'm just gonna rip the band-aid off, alright?"

He sighs, his head falling back, studying the ceiling. "Yes, please just make it quick."

"The women you *date*, again using that term lightly, treat Samantha like shit."

He sits up. I have his full attention now. "What do you mean?"

"They're all nice to her in front of you, but when you're not around or not paying attention, they're mean to her, catty, cruel. Some even use her to get to you, and once they've got you, they turn on her."

"Shit. Well, things just keep getting better for me all around," he whines.

"Hey, asshat, this isn't about you. It's about your sister and your ignorance in not understanding, or being aware of how your actions impact her." I motion to his beer. "Drink up. We're moving on to number three."

"Shit." He takes a long pull of his beer.

I take a sip and set mine on the coffee table. "The chick you were with last night, Veronica Hamm, she's some nasty work. Is she who you disappeared with?"

"Fuck, the fact you know her name at all tells me this is really bad. And yes, she's the one I was with last night, many times actually. She's a wildcat."

"Yeah, well, I sure hope you double bagged as she seems to get around, and just might have some shit that'll make your dick fall off." I'm half-kidding, trying to make him feel bad for his poor choices, but on the same hand, there's no way I would stick my cock in that woman, even tripled bagged.

"Jesus." He withers into the couch a little more. "I was safe, man. Just tell me, what did she do to Sam?"

I'm impressed he at least put two and two together. "Did you know Samantha was seeing some guy named Roger earlier in the year?"

He's back on the edge of the couch. "What? No, she would have told me."

I give him a you're-a-dipshit look. "Really? You talk about guys a lot, do you? Who she has a crush on? What she's been doing on the weekends for the last two years you've been away at college?"

"Fuck me. I'm a total idiot. We talk all the damn time, but...not about guys. I kidded with her yesterday, knowing she didn't have a hot date. She never dates. Yeah, I scared everyone away, but she's all about school and graduating early from college anyways." He puts his head in his hands. "I didn't think she cared about dating."

This sucks. He loves his sister, probably more than anyone else in his life. But he also loves himself a whole lot too, and self-involvement blinds him from seeing what's right in front of him. They don't discuss boys, ever. In his mind, she's his kid sister. He doesn't see her as the sexual creature she is. Though admittedly, if I had a sister, I wouldn't want to think of her in that way either.

Samantha needs him, though. He's her best friend, and if she can't tell this kind of stuff to her best friend, then who is she going to tell?

Nobody. And she deserves better than that.

I do the best I can to ease the news of what happened with Roger and Veronica, but Jace is beside himself, kicking his own ass for having spent the night with such a woman, probably doing the exact same thing she did to Roger, and more.

Much.

Much.

More.

PART 3
ASCENSION

Eight

Joseph

"**D**O YOU EVER SLEEP IN?" I CLOSE THE BACK door.

"Jesus! Joseph." She jumps and nearly spills her coffee. "You scared the crap out of me."

Chuckling, I join her on the double lounger by the pool. "I'm sorry, I thought you would've heard the door open."

"Apparently not." She eyes me sideways under her lashes before setting her mug on the table next to her.

I capture her hand in mine, relishing the warm softness of it. "Let me make it up to you by taking you to lunch."

I didn't get to spend any time with her yesterday. After confronting Jace, we ended up hanging out all day. I've barely even seen her or had a quiet moment with her since we kissed Saturday night, or I guess early yesterday morning.

I need to be sure she's okay. I'm not even sure I'm okay. The vision of my future seems skewed and not nearly as set in stone as it was before. Before meeting Samantha.

"Lunch? You're not hanging out with Jace today?"

"I'd like to hang out with you."

"But…what about Jace?" she persists.

"Do you want me to invite him?"

"I…uh…yes?" She frowns. "No. Actually, I don't."

I brush my lips across the back of her hand. *So soft.* "Good. I don't want to invite him either."

Uncertainty still shines brightly in her eyes. "Won't he wonder…"

"Wonder what? That I'm going to lay you out on the table and make love to you at the restaurant for all to see?"

"Jesus." She gasps and swallows hard as her skin pinkens.

"Sweetness, don't look at me like that. I'm trying to be good here, but when you look at me like you're hungry for me to do just that—I have no hope.

She pulls her hand out of mine. "Then don't say things like that. Put all these ideas in my head. It confuses me."

Confusing is too tame a description for what it's doing to me.

"You're right. I'm sorry. I was trying to make light of the Jace concern. You don't need to worry about Jace. He knows I see you as more than just his sister, but he also knows I respect you enough never to take advantage of you or your age, or your innocence."

She cringes. "Seriously? I'm not some child who doesn't know her own mind. If I wanted to be out getting laid in a restaurant or anywhere else—I would be."

She moves to get up, but I stop her with a gentle hand on her thigh. "Please don't go. I—"

"You and Jace don't get any say in the matter of my *innocence.*"

"I know, and it's not what I meant, exactly. But I hope you won't be doing that. You deserve better than meaningless, casual sex."

"What, it's good enough for you and Jace, but not for me?"

Christ. I scrub my face with my hand. Where did I go wrong here? "Stop. I don't want to fight. I was simply trying to say that Jace trusts me not to lead you astray." I grip her leg. "Stay. Enjoy your coffee, and let's find something else to talk about."

She does as I ask, but I can feel her seething next to me. I'm not sure how to make it better. I just know I need to try. "I'm sorry. Don't be mad."

"I'm not mad." She bites.

My smile is inappropriate at the moment, but I can't help it. She's adorable and sexy when she pouts. "You are. I've offended you, and that was not my intent. Forgive me?"

She softens before my eyes, filling me with relief. "Forgiven. I'm sorry I got upset." She bumps my shoulder.

A wink and a dimpled smile have her smiling back at me. I lean over and kiss her behind her ear.

Her breath catches, and I savor the moment. "Can we just enjoy this for what it is and not have expectations of what it means?"

She shakes her head, raising a brow. "You said I shouldn't do casual."

Fuck, this girl is smart. She could run circles around me.

"You got me there. I'll be honest. You've thrown me for a loop, and I'm a mass of contradictions when it comes to you."

"As long as we're equally off-kilter, I'm okay with that. Let's just enjoy this week with no expectations of more."

I agree, but I fear neither one of us is capable of keeping that promise.

Nine

Samantha

STOLEN GLANCES, COVERT CONTACT, AND SECRET desires have me in a tizzy. My mind is reeling; my heart racing, and I'm aching in places I didn't know I could. For the last hour Joseph has been torturing me.

Pure. Evil. Torture.

It started out sweet and innocent enough. Margot and Jace picked the movie, or movies, to be more precise. We're having an *Aliens* marathon, apparently. Jace and I have seen all of them, but never back to back. We're on the second movie, and somewhere between when the first one ended and the second started, Joseph scooted closer to me on the couch, the sides of our bodies touching from my shoulder, down my arm, to my hip, and the length of my thigh. His hand moves to touch my hand resting on my thigh. Just the barest of touches, and it sends my heart thundering, more so than the terrifying alien that just ripped apart that poor actor on the screen.

Joseph links his pinkie with mine as he presses the entire side of his hard, warm body against me.

I glance up at him, his stare heating my skin even further.

"You okay?" he whispers a hair's breadth from my mouth.

I nod, swallowing stiffly as he licks his lips, his gaze focused on my mouth.

"You sure you don't need anything?" His lips brush my ear. "Anything at all?"

Jesus.

"I'm fine." I keep my blurry gaze trained on the movie, not seeing anything but the vision of his pouty lips too close to mine.

For the next hour, his hand moves to caress the top of my hand in slow circles. Then he places my hand on his thigh and his hand on my thigh, where he continues that same slow circling motion. All the while we remain facing forward. Jace and Margot are on twin recliners turned toward the TV, oblivious to the torture taking place behind them.

And now he slings his arm over the back of the couch, his fingers running along the curve of my neck and down my shoulder as far as he can go and still be touching my skin around my scoop-neck t-shirt, and then back up to the ridge of my ear and to my earlobe. Over and over again he tortures me. My mind is addled with wanton need and my panties soaked beyond repair.

Unable to take a moment more, I pop up off the couch, making Joseph jump. "Popcorn! I'm going to make popcorn. Anyone need anything?" I scurry off to the kitchen, barely giving them a chance to give me their drink requests.

Instead of tackling the task at hand, I pause at the kitchen window. The pool shimmers in the moonlight with aqua ripples as the pool genie glides through the water, silently doing its job to keep the water clean and pure. It's soothing, and I find myself taking deep, relaxing breaths.

A shiver runs up my spine, tightening my already sensitized nipples. My body alerting me to his presence before I'm cogently aware.

His lips graze my neck, taking the same path as his fingers did mere moments ago. His arms engulf me as his body molds to my back.

My head naturally falls to his chest and my eyes roll closed as he grazes my nipples with his thumbs. His lips pay homage to my neck and jaw, and finally my mouth as he pivots enough to consume me.

I'm lost in him, too lost, too consumed.

Before either one of us can come to our senses, I hear a gasp from behind him.

Joseph grumbles as his lips separate from mine.

Margot stands in the doorway, her eyes wide with shock. "I'm s… sorry," she struggles to speak and starts to back out of the kitchen.

"Don't go," Joseph says.

He kisses me with a soft *smack*. "Never enough, Sweetness." He then saunters out of the kitchen in the opposite direction of the den.

I wonder if he's going to go jerk off. For a split second, I consider joining him.

"So, I guess it's safe to say Joe doesn't see you as Jace's kid sister." Margot draws my attention back to her smiling, gloating face.

"Don't. It doesn't mean anything," I whisper for fear of Jace joining us in the kitchen.

"It sure looks like it meant *something*." She fans her face. "That was hot."

It was. It truly was. I sigh and grab two bags of microwave popcorn from the pantry. "It's not going anywhere, though. So, I'd rather not analyze the hell out of it."

She grabs a bag from me, pulling off the plastic wrapper and placing it in the microwave to pop. "That's not like you, Sam. You speculate and consider things from all angles. *Analyze-the-shit-out-of-things* is your middle name."

God, I love her. I wrap her in a hug. "We're just going to enjoy it while it lasts. It's just now. Nothing more. Okay?" I release her, avoiding looking at her.

She spots my watery eyes anyway and gently touches my shoulder. "Bull winkles, Sam. You really like him."

I place the popcorn bowl on the counter. "I do."

"You're gonna get hurt," she says softly.

I tap my temple. "I'm trying to keep it up here…" I then touch my heart. "…and keep it far away from here. I refuse to fall off the deep end and swoon like a silly teenager over my big brother's college roommate, who also just happens to be the future VP of the company I'd die to work for, and will apparently be my boss if that dream comes true."

"Holy nut cracker," she exclaims, her mouth agape and her large brown eyes even larger, if that's even possible.

"Yep, that about sums it up. I'd rather not think about it." I hand her the bowl of popcorn. "Take this, go back in and watch the movie. I'll be in, in a minute."

She nods, still in shock. "I love you, Sam."

I hand her her drink with a large smile. "I love you too. Now go act like you know nothing."

"Got it." With a quick nod, she departs the kitchen.

I grab the other drinks and take them to the den, setting them down, and then hurry upstairs for a fresh pair of panties.

I exit my bedroom as Joseph is about to descend the stairs.

He stops when he spots me. "Hey, what are you doing up here?" He looks flushed and guilty, like I caught him with his hand in the cookie jar. I may have hit the mark on my assumption.

I motion over my shoulder to my room. "I…" *Shit. What do I say?*

And now that I'm floundering, his interest just piqued. "Don't smirk at me. It's your fault I had to go change my panties."

He groans. "Christ, Samantha. Don't tell me that." He stalks closer, backing me up to the wall.

"And what exactly were you doing?" I press my hands against his chest to keep him from touching me, but it's a lost cause.

His hands fist my shirt at my waist, and his forehead lowers to mine. "Exactly what I'll have to go back and do again if you tell me I made you wet enough to require a change of panties."

His voice is thick and deep with need, causing my stomach to flutter. I lift up and press my lips to his. "Did you think of me?"

"Fuck," he grinds out, pressing me against the wall. "With every long, hard stroke I thought of only you."

Shit.

He cups my breast and holds my jaw. "Will you think of me as you touch yourself later? Will you picture my mouth sucking your nipples, as my fingers slide through your wet pussy, teasing and circling your clit until you cry out my name and come for me?"

Holy hell, that's the hottest thing I've ever heard, and I'm not sure if it's the words, his gravelly voice, his erection pressing against my stomach, or the fact that he just jerked off thinking of me, and now he's hard again. But whatever it is, I'm going to need another change of panties.

"If I wasn't going to before, I'm definitely going to now." I'm shaking with need and want nothing more than to ask him to do all of that to me right now.

Instead, I bust out laughing.

He drops his hands and edges back enough to see me fully.

"Did you really just masturbate thinking of me? And are seriously considering doing it again?" I press my hand to my mouth to try to silence my laughter, but it's of little use. I slide down the wall as my legs can't support me in their weakened state.

"Yes, I did. And yes, I was planning on doing it again, but now that you're laughing at me, it's kinda killing the mood." He slides down the opposite wall, staring at me.

"I'm sorry." I giggle.

He reaches for my hand, squeezing it tightly. "It's okay."

"Don't get me wrong. It was really hot. It just struck me as funny and maybe a little sad." My laughter finally abates. "We can't keep doing this, Joseph. We're just going to frustrate each other to no end." I glance down the hall towards the steps. "You were driving me crazy on the couch, such little touches, but what they did to me—there was nothing little about it."

His graces me with his sexy dimpled smile. "It was driving me crazy too. That's why I followed you into the kitchen. I just can't seem to stay away. It's like a live wire that keeps pulling at me, beckoning me to you."

"That's crazy sweet, and it's the same for me. But I think we need to try to resist it. Margot busting us is bad enough. What if it had been my parents, then what?"

"Agreed." He stands up, offering his hand, and pulls me to my feet and then into his arms. His lips brush across mine with one final kiss, as if to seal the deal. "But make no mistake, I'm still going to get off thinking of you."

"I find that oddly complimentary." I giggle.

"Good, you should." He releases me and starts down the hall but stops when he realizes I'm not following. "Are you coming?"

I raise a brow at his double entendre.

He laughs when he realizes what he said. "You know what I mean."

"Yes, I do." I motion to my bedroom door. "I'll be down in a minute." I bite my lip to stop from laughing again.

"Christ. You're gonna kill me with this panty thing."

"Hey, it's your fault."

He chuckles. "And I'll gladly take credit for it." He comes back and kisses me, sweet and tenderly. "I'll see you downstairs, Sweetness."

Joseph

I shuffle through the house Tuesday morning, trying to avoid Samantha. Margot spent the night, and I don't know if she's still here. But, if she is, I should leave them to that girl bonding time woman seem to like so much.

Jace and I head out to the gym and catch a late breakfast at our favorite diner near the hospital. It's open 24/7 and is popular with the hospital staff, college kids, and anyone with the munchies or hangovers.

"Margot's a trip. She likes to give you shit." I take a bite of my loaded egg scramble. "I like her."

Jace chuckles, adding more syrup to his stack of banana walnut pancakes. "Yes, she does. She has a younger brother at home, and they rib each other in the same way." He downs his orange juice. "She's good people. Had a bit of a hard start in life, but she doesn't let it get her down."

"What do you mean?"

"She had some health issues when she was a kid. She's fine, but she's one tough cookie. She's got a backbone of steel, that one." His gaze remains on his empty glass thoughtfully. "She's good for Sam. She brings out Sam's silly side, doesn't let her be so serious all the time."

"I've noticed that about Samantha. She's rather introspective, self-reliant. Has she always been that way?" I'm curious on his take on why she's so *together*.

He forks a mouthful, making me believe he's going to eat instead of answering, but he sets his fork down and meets my stare. "I don't really know. I think she comes by it naturally from Mom. But Sam takes it to another level. She's always been a loner, never really *seemed* to need anything or anyone. When she was old enough to read, she'd disappear for hours. When it came to birthday parties, she'd shy away from being the center of attention. I think her tenth birthday was the last party she had. She begged my mom to stop throwing them. She only wanted to celebrate with family, quietly at home."

He takes another bite of food, his forehead creased. I believe he has more to share.

I eat and patiently wait.

It's a few more mouthfuls from each of us before he speaks again. "She's shy, and yet she's not. She's truly bold when she has something to say. It's not that she can't talk to people or have fun…it's more like…she chooses not to. I've wondered if it's my fault. That I was too large and over the top, too busy being the center of attention, sucking all of the oxygen out of the room and leaving none for her." His eyes sadden as he looks at me. "I've been a shit brother to her."

I wish I could say I disagree, but I find much of what he says is probable. "It's not too late to change your dynamic. You'll always be bigger than life, and there's nothing wrong with that. She'll always be the steady rock behind you, but you can help her shine."

"Yeah." He smiles. "I could do that. I don't want her to feel like what she has to offer isn't enough and try to change. And I'm worried I've done just that with my ignorance and self-importance."

Yep, couldn't have said it better myself.

When we get back to their house, I pause at the bottom of the stairs. Music is blaring from somewhere on the first floor.

Jace continues up the stairs. "Sam must be in the library working." He looks back at me as I follow, in need of a shower. "She listens to music to clear her head. It helps her focus."

"How can she focus with it that loud?" I muse, looking over my shoulder as if I can see through the walls to the library.

He laughs. "She only listens to it loud until she feels her creative juices flowing, and then she turns it off."

Ah. Okay, that makes sense. Kinda.

After my shower, I brave the pelting onslaught of music still coming from the library. My laptop bag in hand, I slowly open the library door, feeling like an intruder in her private space.

I slip inside and close the door. It takes me a second to spot her in the back of the room in front of rows and rows of built-in bookshelves made of mahogany. The color reminds me of Samantha's hair, which is currently pinned on top of her head. Tendrils escape their confinement as she bounces, sways, and...grinds to the reggae song currently playing.

My lips curl in an unfettered smile as I lean against the nearest wall, watching in amused enjoyment. She does love her music. I knew that from dancing with her last Saturday night, but this right here is something entirely liberating. I feel bad for watching such unabashed freedom coming from a woman who is normally self-conscious of all things about herself. I should turn away, but I can't. I'm transfixed, mesmerized by the sway of her hips, the flow of her arms, and the utter joy on her face. She. Is. Beautiful.

One foot in front of the other, on instinct, I find myself drawing closer, like a honeybee to its amber pot of liquid gold.

Her movements slow as she turns, coming to a complete stop when her eyes lock on me in complete horror.

I grab hold of her upper arms, pulling her to me. "Don't freak out." I speak into her ear, ensuring she can hear me. "Don't you dare feel embarrassed. That was the sexiest thing I've ever seen. I enjoyed every second, every movement, every last breath and beat of your passionate heart. And I want to experience it again and again." I stand straight and breathe in relief to see a smile on her lips that sparkles in her eyes. "Beautiful."

"Thank you." She grabs a remote off the bookshelf and turns down the music.

"What song is that, anyway?"

"It's 'Say Hey' by Michael Franti & Spearhead. Do you like it?"

"I love it. I'll have to download it immediately."

She moves to the desk where her laptop sits and downs a large gulp of water. "What are you up to?"

I retrieve my laptop from the floor near the door. "I thought I'd join you, if you don't mind. I have some work to do for MCI and thought we could keep each other company. I assume you're working on your paper?"

"Yeah. I'm nearly done. I was taking a break, clearing my head."

I smile at that. "Yes, Jace told me you use music to do that."

"I do. It helps me get out of my head and find a creative space that allows my thoughts, words to flow more freely." Thankfully, there's not an ounce of remorse in her voice or manner.

"I can see how that might work. I may have to try it sometime."

"Good. Then I'll get to watch you dance and lose yourself to the music." She beams.

I shake my head, chuckling. "I'm afraid you far exceed me in grace, skill, and pure passion."

She rakes me up and down with her eyes. "I don't believe that for a second."

"Someday, we'll compare notes," I promise.

I set my laptop up at the table across the room from her. I'd like to share her desk, but I need to make a phone call to my Uncle Max, and I don't want to be overly intrusive on her space. She digs back into her paper, fingers typing away, and I peruse the reports my uncle sent me.

Five reports reviewed, two phone calls, and an hour later I look up as Samantha sets a Coke on the table next to me.

"Thank you." I take a cool sip.

"You're welcome." She points to my laptop. "Do you have much longer?"

"I'm finished actually. How about you?"

She leans against the table. "I'm done for today. I was thinking of making dinner and wondered if you wanted to keep me company. Unless you have plans tonight."

"Nope, no plans." I shut my laptop. "I'm all yours. What'd you have in mind?"

"Okay, don't laugh. I thought it might be fun to make pizzas and have a game night: board games or cards, nothing electronic. My parents love that sort of thing, and secretly, so does Jace. Are you up for it?"

I'm up for anything this girl offers me. "Absolutely."

Ten

Samantha

I STILL AS I ENTER THE DEN, NOT REALIZING JOSEPH is on the phone or in the room at all. I thought he was upstairs hanging out with Jace. I start to back out of the room when he glances up and stops me with a radiant smile. He holds up one finger, asking me to wait.

"Yeah, I will," he says, going silent as his eyes peruse me from head to toe and he listens to the person on the other line.

I squirm under his examination, but his frown stills my fidgeting.

"I talked to them earlier. They're having a good time, but no, I'm not sorry I didn't go. I've had a great time with the Cavanaghs. I've enjoyed getting to know Samantha and their parents better. Yes. Yes, she is." His smile turns sultry as he stands and stalks closer, changing to speakerphone. "How come nobody ever told me how beautiful she is?"

"You noticed?" The male voice on the other line says, followed by a deep chuckle.

"How could I not?" Joseph cups my cheek. "She's amazing," he nearly whispers.

He's talking to someone about me? About. Me? My heart skips a beat as his head lowers to mine. "I have to go, Dad. Give Mom my love. Tell her I'm sorry I missed her."

"I love you, son."

Joseph's lips feather across mine. "I love you too." His eyes burn with things unsaid.

I fight the panic exploding inside me. I know he's talking to his dad, but the look in his eyes seems like he's saying it to me. Impossible.

"You look beautiful," he says as he ends the call and slips the phone into his pocket. "Like an early Christmas present I want to unwrap."

"Joseph," I plead for him to not be so nice to me. To not get my hopes up that this is more than it is.

"I know. Give me a kiss. Help me make it through the day without your lips on mine."

He doesn't wait for my reply. He didn't need to. His lips crash into mine with the force of the gods, or so it seems. My knees go weak, and he moans as he steadies me in his strong embrace, his mouth savoring me like the Thanksgiving meal we are about to consume.

A deep voice clears their throat from behind me.

Shit.

"Sir." Joseph nods with a smile over my head.

I turn to see my dad smiling at us. "It's time to eat, pumpkin." His eyes flit between the two of us, and then with a wink he's gone.

"Shit," I say out loud this time. "Why the hell are you *smiling?*"

Joseph kisses my cheek. "It's okay. Your dad and I talked."

"What?" I'm completely horrified.

"It's okay, Samantha. He knows there's something here, but that we *choose* to not pursue anything right now."

If that's supposed to make me feel better, it doesn't. He told my dad he likes me, but not enough to be with me, like I'm some chick he's diddling on his break from college.

I push away and stomp to the kitchen, furious for letting myself think I was otherwise.

Joseph

That didn't go well. I don't understand why she's so upset. She'd probably be really pissed if she knew what I really thought and what I'm planning. I thought being upfront with her father was the best way to go. To speak my intentions for the future. I was trying to smooth the way for us, own it, instead of continuing to slink around like two lust-riddled teenagers, though in truth that's the way I feel when I'm near her. Which was even more reason to be sure her father understands I'm not here to mess around with her, to use her and leave her high and dry.

"I can see you have an inkling of the kind of woman Samantha will be. It's important to me that she fulfills her dreams. She has a passion for what she wants, but at the same time, she's afraid to want it—to believe it's possible. She's a contradiction unto herself. She needs a man strong enough to stand beside her and not in front of her," Daniel said to me as we grocery shopped yesterday while Samantha and her mom stayed home making pies and preparing for today.

"I understand, Sir. I would never want to stand in her way or be the reason she doesn't become who she's meant to be. That's why I want to wait to pursue anything with her until she's out of college. Two and a half years, if she finishes by her timeline. I need that time too, to focus on graduating and assume my role at MCI."

It's the perfect plan. But it's a plan I can't share with her. I don't want her to put her life on hold for me. She needs to get out there and experience life. If I tell her about my two-point-five-year plan, she'd wait for me, and I don't want that. I want her to date, get to know what she likes, who she is so she comes to me because she wants *me*, not because I'm the first guy who came along. She knows who she is when it comes to school and her career, but she doubts herself as a woman. She needs to find her footing. She needs to experiment. Find who she is beyond the 5.0 GPA high school student, or the dean's list college student, or the stellar MCI employee she is destined to be. Who is Samantha without those things?

I see her, but does she?

I grip the back of my neck and squeeze. "Fuck." I sigh as I follow Samantha into the kitchen to see what I can do to soothe her hurt feelings, but everyone's ready to eat and I don't get the chance to speak to her.

"Sam said you spoke to your family. How are they enjoying their vacations?" Eleanor asks me after we sit down to eat.

"My brothers are out on a boat today, deep sea fishing. Having a blast. They'll be having fish, or whatever they catch for dinner." I glance at Samantha on my left. She's picking at her food, barely eating. That just won't do. I slide my hand to her thigh and grip it firmly.

She tries to dislodge my hand, but I grab hers instead and hold it tightly. She needs to hear what I'm saying and stop listening to the devil in her head. "My parents are enjoying skiing. I only got to talk to my dad as Mom's having a spa day while he hits the slopes. There's a big dinner at the lodge tonight."

"Ah, that's nice," Eleanor exclaims. "Do you miss being with them for the holiday?"

I squeeze Samantha's hand. "I thought I would, but it's been so nice here." I look around the table at each of them. Samantha meets my gaze as I stop on her. "I've really enjoyed this week. It feels like home too," I say to her, and I hope she hears me.

"We've enjoyed having you, son," Daniel says as he serves himself more turkey. "Eleanor, my love, you've outdone yourself. This turkey is nearly as succulent as you are."

"Dad!" Sam blushes.

"Ugh, seriously!" Jace exclaims with a groan and a roll of his eyes.

Daniel winks at his wife with a laugh, and then holds up his wine glass. "To the most amazing woman I know, the love of my life, the mother of my children, and the keeper of my heart." He clinks glasses with her and all of us, but then his eyes return to his wife. "I love you, woman."

Eleanor's eyes glisten, and she leans forward, meeting his lips halfway. "I love you more than life itself, Daniel. Thank you for this life, every day passed, and every day yet to come."

They take a drink of their wine, never taking their eyes off each other.

Christ. That's some love affair they have. I feel like we should leave the room.

Samantha leans over. "You'll get used to it." She smiles at me, but her eyes are sad and filled with tears she's fighting to tame.

Someday, Sweetness, is all I can think as the lump in my throat keeps me silent. I simply nod, squeeze and then release her hand so that she can eat.

I never dreamt I'd find a woman who's so obviously made for me. Perfect in her imperfections I have yet to discover, but whole-heartedly can't wait to unveil.

PART 4
BEST INTENTIONS

Eleven

Joseph

I T'S BEEN AN AMAZING WEEK. JACE AND I LEAVE IN A few hours to drive home to Austin for school starting back tomorrow. I'll be sad to see Dallas in my rearview mirror because this time I'll be leaving a girl who's held me captive for the last nine days…and forever, if I play my cards right.

I stalk through the house searching for her, finding her where I should have checked in the first place, in the library. I've come to realized it's her "office" as such. Her study pad. Her think tank. Her sanctuary. She's at home here, at peace among the shelves of books, cozy couches, with her laptop buzzing along as her nimble fingers stroke each key succinctly and with lightning speed.

The door is open, so there is no noise to announce my presence as I stop at the threshold to take her in. As happens every time I draw near, the air between us thickens and sizzles, coming alive as if it's a third party in the room, not a barrier between us, but a bridge, a direct connection from my soul to hers. If I could see energy, I imagine the air between us would be as colorful as our auras themselves, an extension of us, linking me to her, reflecting our moods, our emotions, our passion. She lights me up at the mere sight of her. If fire were an aura, it would be mine when I'm in her presence: hot red, yellow, orange, blue flames dancing around my body, licking the air, eating it up between us, consuming the oxygen, drawing her to me so I. Can. Breathe.

Her fingers slow, coming to a halt as she senses me. Her face lifts from the screen, zooming in on my location.

My breath hitches, and my blood races to the part of me that wants to claim her.

Down, boy.

"Joseph." Her silken lips move. I don't hear the word so much as I feel it.

My body's in motion before my brain even makes the command. *Need.* I close the distance between us before it grows in the hours ahead.

She stands. Her hand lifts to her chest, and she backs away. There's no fear on her remarkable face. All I see is her desire reflecting mine, and it's the sheer force of it hitting her before I physically touch her. It's the same for me except it draws me to her, eliciting proactive motion to her reactive stance.

"Sweetness." My lips clash with hers as my arms envelop her.

She wraps around me in sweet perfection.

Mine.

Hers.

Yin.

Yang.

One.

Christ, I can't even make sense of my feelings, much less the depth of my words as they swirl in my head as our tongues touch…captivating the other. Our kiss is focused, drawing each other in, in hypnotizing passion.

Her hands scorch my skin as they move along my back and then up my chest to take root in my hair. A slight tug elicits a growl from me, forcing me in motion again. I cup her ass, lifting her, and like my true other half, she wraps her legs around me as I walk us to the secluded couch away from the door I should have shut when I entered the room.

Seated with her straddling my lap, I pull her close. My kisses slow to savor instead of devour. I need to concentrate and focus on remembering the feel of her, the smell of her, the all-consuming essence of her.

"Joseph," she moans against my lips, and I can hear the ache in her heart.

She's with me. She feels it too.

Thank god.

She's kissing me as much as I'm kissing her, taking and giving, beginning and ending, unhinging and completing.

Mine.

She grinds against my hard-on, her need taking over her senses and nearly overriding mine. Nearly.

"Christ, Samantha." My hands grip her hips to stop her movements. When she stills I kiss her one more time, my hand sliding to her nape, holding her close as our lips separate.

Pressing my forehead to hers, my breaths are harsh with need. "We need to talk."

She sighs, trying to pull away, but my hand keeps her in place.

"Nothing good ever comes from those four words."

I chuckle at the truth of that statement. "I'm hoping we can find some good in them. Maybe not immediately, but down the road, we will be better off for having spoken them."

Her hand wraps around my wrist. "Okay, but can you let me go?"

"No, Sweetness, that's just it. I can't."

"That's not what I meant," she says softly.

I release her, and she slowly sits back, my grip on her thighs ensuring she doesn't move any farther. "I know what you meant." The sadness on her face matches the sorrow in my heart which has a death-like grip on my chest. "We've been skirting this all week, playing with fire, but it's time we speak the truth and the reality of the situation."

"I got it," she says hoarsely, trying to stand up. She's sliding her walls back into place. I can't blame her. She needs to protect her heart as much as I have a need to protect her.

I grip her tighter. "Please don't pull away. Stay with me." I turn her face toward mine with a hand on her jaw so I can kiss her, remind her of what I'm feeling, open her back up for just a few moments more.

She sighs and relaxes in my arms, giving herself over to me once again.

This time when I end the kiss, I pull so her head rests on my shoulder and mine in the crook of her neck. "Don't shut me out just yet. Let me say what needs to be said before you disappear back into yourself."

The sound of anguish meeting my ears guts me. Her grip around my neck and shoulders tightens. I can feel her trying to rein in her emotions, stopping any further sounds from escaping. Yet, I can feel the warm tears on my neck. I hold her tighter, running my hand along her back, trying to give her comfort when I know I'm the cause of her pain. "I'm sorry. If I were a stronger man, we wouldn't be in this boat, but as it stands I'm trying to do the right thing, for both our sakes."

She nods, her voice shaking when she speaks. "I could have resisted you. Been stronger. But I didn't want to."

"I said I'm sorry. And I am sorry for making you cry, but I'm not sorry about you not resisting me. I've never felt this connection before. It's fast and intense. We need to think and put things in perspective. We're both intelligent people, we need to use our brains and not our hearts at the moment."

My girl takes a deep breath, and slowly releases me, sitting up to wipe her tears and sniffle. She's adorable and sexy all at the same time. I cup her cheek, running my thumb along the dampness. "I don't want to hurt you. I don't want to be a distraction for you. We both have school to focus on, and our careers."

She takes another deep breath, letting it out slowly and nods her agreement.

I lean in to kiss her. One. More. Time.

Samantha

He's only been gone six hours, but the longer he's gone, the more my mind falls back to old ways and disregards the words he said, the emotions he expressed. My mind twists the intention of us not pursuing a relationship into him not ever really wanting me.

I try to hold on to his words, the intent of his words, but it's like a dream that fades the longer I'm awake. I remember what the dream was about, but I can't verbalize it in any concrete way, and the more I think about it, the more muddled it becomes.

What stays true is the memory of the feel of him against my body. The way I felt in his arms. Safe. Desired. Home. Free.

I didn't have to pretend with him or feel I had expectations I had to live up to. I could just be me. The me who's confident in my skills, in my studies, and in my ability to do what is needed to get a task done and get it done correctly. But I was also free to be the uncertain me, the one who's vulnerable and doesn't always want to be the most responsible person in the room.

But that's all a dream, and the dream has ended.

It's time to focus back on school and my career aspirations. I'll allow myself a fantasy or two of Joseph being my first, of giving him my body. That should turn me on, but it makes me even sadder to think of what we had as only physical and nothing more. I want him to want me for more than just the pleasure my body can give him.

In an effort to shake it off, I head to the kitchen for a snack and then back to the library to work on my term paper. It's done, but it could always use another read-through to catch any details missing or grammatical errors.

Everything, no matter how much it's worked on, can always be improved upon.

Except Joseph. He's perfect the way he is.

I'm doomed.

I sigh and try to shake him from my thoughts.

On my way back to the library, I stop at the entryway to the den. My parents are cuddled up on the couch watching an old movie, the same couch Joseph had me tied up in lusty knots on only six days ago during our *Aliens* movie night. A fire is burning; the lights are low, and they're cocooned under a blanket. Mom nuzzles under Dad's chin. He gently cups her face and kisses her head. He whispers something to her that makes her smile and sink in deeper.

That.

Right. There.

Is.

My.

Dream.

PART 5
UNTIL YOU

DECEMBER

Twelve

Joseph

'M A MESS. I'M A FUCKING MESS.

Until I met her, I never had trouble concentrating. Keeping my head in the game. Keeping my goal of school first, play second.

But since spending Thanksgiving with Samantha, my head is all scrambled. My heart is all tied up. My thoughts are not my own.

I try.

Christ, I try to push her to the back of my mind, busy myself with school work, working out, drinking.

Way too much drinking. I have to knock that shit out.

Plus, when I drink, my resolve to not call her, text her, see her, starts to crumble.

Many times I've had to leave my phone in my car, just to reduce the temptation, make it more difficult to give in.

Jace isn't helping much, either. He doesn't know what's tying me up inside. He doesn't know what happened at Thanksgiving, that his sister and I kissed, touched...had a thing. My cock gets hard just thinking of it. Thinking of her.

In general, Jace knows I can't afford to get involved right now; my focus has to be school and my career at MCI. He knows I see his sister as someone in my future, potentially, but I haven't confided in him about my plan to wait until after she's out of college and then come for her. Hell, maybe he thought I was speaking in generalities and that I meant someone *like* Samantha would be perfect for me. I'm not correcting that assumption. I can't take the chance that he'll tell her.

It's not that she won't fit into my life. She will fit in, perfectly. It's all about timing, and ours sucks balls. She needs to finish high school and college. She needs time to experience life—to find herself as a woman. I need to finish college.

She'll be heading to Austin, and a year later I'll move back to Dallas to work with my family at MCI.

We're out of sync. And it won't be changing anytime soon.

Two and a half years. Then I'm coming for her—no holds barred.

Just because I've made my choice doesn't mean I'm not tempted to reach out to her. It's a daily struggle, and it sucks.

Just as I'm about to give in to temptation to see how she is, just to hear her lovely voice, there's a knock at the front door.

I tuck my phone away and answer the door. "Fin? What are you doing here?"

He laughs. "It's good to see you too, brother."

"Shit, I'm sorry." I step aside. "Come in."

I follow him to the living room. "It's good to see you. I'm just surprised, that's all."

He shrugs. "Yeah. I thought about giving you a heads-up, but I knew you'd come up with some excuse for me not to come."

He's right, I would've blown him off, made up some school project, downplayed my heartache to wallow alone in misery.

"Where's Jace?"

I take a seat on the couch, motioning for Fin to do the same. Not like I need to make him feel at home. He lived in this house before me. "He's on a date."

Fin's eyebrows shoot up. "Really? Like a real date, or is that a new euphemism for dinner and a blowjob?"

"A real date. He's trying to turn over a new leaf since Thanksgiving. Less manwhoring. More…dating."

"Huh." He contemplates the idea. "Well, good for him." His eyes circle the room before landing back on me. "And you? Are you dating?"

I let out a breath and sink down into the couch. "You know I'm not."

"Because of Sam." He straightens his tie even though it's not even a millimeter out of place.

I sit forward, my elbows resting on my knees. "I told you—the timing is off."

"Hmm." He nods. "But you're not dating anyone else either."

"I don't want anyone else, Fin."

I've talked to him about Samantha. He knows the score, how I feel about her, what I see as our future.

"So, you're what? Going to be celibate for the next few years then?" He shifts to settle into the couch more, like he's getting comfortable for a drawn-out conversation.

I'm not up for that. I scrub my face with my hand. "I don't know, Fin. All I know is she's the only girl I want. Now. Tomorrow. Ever. It would feel like I'm cheating on her."

Cheating myself.

He observes me dryly. "*You* don't want to commit to her. You don't want *her* to commit to you. But you don't plan on dating other people." His eyes narrow with skepticism. "Isn't that commitment?"

Fucking Fin. Leave it to him to point out the obvious.

I don't respond. What would I say? *Yes?*

We head out for dinner at one of his favorite hangouts, nothing fancy. Good burgers, good beer, and good music.

"You never did say. What brings you to town?" I take a bite of my burger and wash it down with the last of my beer.

Fin has a way of looking at me like he loves me, but I'm not necessarily the smartest cracker in the box. It's a *we're-just-thankful-he-dresses-himself* kind of look. "I came for you, dumbass. Why else would I be here?"

Really?

I feel like I can breathe a little easier with him here to help me pass the time. The weekends are the hardest. It's been three weeks since I've seen Samantha. Three weeks too long, and yet time is not passing fast enough. I don't know how I'll survive another week of this, much less years. At this rate, I'll go crazy before we're both out of school and free to pursue a relationship.

I shrug. "Honestly? I didn't think you'd come here for me."

His open hand whacks me on the side of the head. "You're smarter than this. It must be the blue balls affecting your brain function. You need me to get you set up with some porn and a cock-sucking toy?"

I laugh out loud. "Cock-sucking toy? Will it be from your own personal collection?"

"Fuck, no. It would be from Matt's. I don't have any need for that shit."

I scoff. "What and Matt does? That boy gets so much action there's no way he jerks off, there aren't enough hours in the day."

We both nearly double over in laughter.

Damn it feels good to laugh.

After our laughter dies down and another beer is consumed, I decide to bring up an issue that's been bothering me for weeks now, but I didn't want to discuss over the phone. "Why didn't you tell me Samantha interned at MCI last summer and has plans to return next summer, and to get a job with us after she graduates? She wants to work in *my* department. Don't you think I should have known that?"

Usually composed Fin flinches as if I punched him. "I knew this was going to come back to bite me in the ass." He sighs, putting down his beer. "You're right. I should have told you. Trusted you enough to handle it with decorum. But the other side of that coin is—you aren't VP yet, and Uncle Max agreed, given your friendship with Jace—and Sam's request to fly under the radar—that perhaps there was no harm in letting it slide."

My same green eyes stare back at me as I contemplate. "I can see your point. But it still pisses me off."

He nods. "I know, but would you be nearly as pissed if you didn't care for her like you do? If it were just one of your other friends' kid sisters, would you be so upset?"

He has a point. "No," I admit.

"Plus, Jace asked us not to tell her who you were either. According to him, she's dreamed of working for MCI since she was just a kid. It meant the world to her to have gotten the internship. He didn't want her to think he or you had anything to do with it. Admittingly, you two being roommates and Sam being head over heels for MCI is already an amazing coincidence on its own. Add in the fact she got an internship at sixteen, ahead of other older candidates, makes it difficult to believe. Though, all true. It was a cluster-fuck of secrets all woven to be sure she got no special treatment."

I think back to the look on her face when she told me about her dream of working for MCI since she saw that news story when she was just ten years old. She lit up like a kid on Christmas morning, a look that makes my heart ache for her even more. "She loves MCI like it's her family heritage too."

Fin nods. "Maybe it's supposed to be. She wouldn't have needed the strings anyways. She was a rising star, received rave reviews from her manager, and was instrumental in getting two of our new key products out of research and development and into production."

I feel a wave of pride in hearing that.

Fin shakes his head. "She even has a couple of phone apps she developed and sells."

I knew she was smart and technology-minded, but not to the level Fin describes.

It irks me that I didn't know. But in the end, I understand the need to do things on her own. If I had known Jace's sister was working there, I would have searched her out and helped her in any way I could.

"Are we good, brother?" Fin asks.

"Of course. Just don't keep things from me again, especially when it comes to her."

"Understood."

Another round of beers and another hour of laughter later, Fin nods to a table in the corner. "I think you've got an admirer. The dark-haired chick over there can't keep her eyes off you. It's too bad. She's more my type than yours."

"You're in luck then, as I'm off the market."

He takes a sip of beer. "You're going to have to tell her that. She's on her way over here, and she's brought a friend." His smile is devious.

Great. Just what I need.

"Joe?" A soft voice greets me from behind before coming to stand beside me.

"Margot?" My insides light up. Samantha's not here, but I can't help feeling a little closer to her at the sight of Margot. "Hey. How are you? What are you doing in Austin?"

I only met Margot once over Thanksgiving when she busted Samantha and I kissing. Other than the cockblocking, she seemed like a nice person. It was obvious they've all known each other for a long time with how well she fit into their family dynamic. Especially how she busted Jace's balls like the rest of us do.

"I'm good. I'm here visiting my sister." She gestures to the woman standing next to her. "Jenny, this is Joe. He's Jace's roommate and Sam's… uh…hmm…friend, too."

I cringe at that introduction, but understand her uncertainty. It kills me she can't introduce me as Samantha's boyfriend.

I stand, sticking my hand out to Jenny. "It's nice to meet you. This is my brother Fin."

Fin's transfixed on Margot, giving me pause before I continue. "Fin, this is Margot. She's a good friend of Samantha's."

He's already on his feet and shakes hands with Margot and her sister. "It's nice to meet you both."

His eyes wander back to Margot.

Too thin for my tastes, but right up Fin's alley. She's quite pretty, with delicate features, except her huge light brown eyes are almost too large for her face. Her sister has similar features, but is curvier with green eyes.

"Would you like to join us?" Fin and I offer at the same time.

I can't wait to give him shit about this later.

Samantha

"You did what?" I screech on the phone and cringe at the volume of my voice.

"When I was visiting Jenny. We actually had drinks with him and his brother Fin."

I'm shocked. I knew she was going to visit her sister this past weekend, but I never thought for a second she would run into Joseph.

Why didn't she tell me sooner? That was a week ago!

I have a million questions I want to ask. But I can't go there. I can't afford to think of him more than I already do. It's been difficult since he and Jace headed home to Austin after Thanksgiving. I miss him. I miss Joseph. We spent almost every day together. We tried not to give in to the invisible pull making us gravitate toward each other. Even when I wasn't looking at him, I could feel him. I could feel his presence. His eyes on me. His desire for me.

Me.

Like. I. Was. His.

There was a tether between us that grew tighter with distance and eased when we were close. It seemed to correlate to the tightness in my chest and the knot in my stomach. When he was near, all was good. When he was not, I felt like I was coming apart at the seams.

My body started to rely on his to feel at peace. To function properly. *Crazy. Beyond. Crazy.*

Now, nearly a month later I still ache. My body craves what it can't have. My mind wanders to what my heart wants, what my soul desires, what my essence can't seem to ignore. When we said we weren't a permanent thing, I'd meant it…I tried to mean it, but a part of me hoped he'd call and tell me he'd made a mistake and wanted more. When that didn't happen, I'd hoped for even a flirty text. He didn't even bother giving me that.

Joseph will only break my heart. I need to move on.

"Sam?" Margot's voice cuts through my musings.

"Sorry. I'm here. So, how is Jenny? Did you have a good visit?"

The line is silent for a moment. Is she contemplating whether she should tell me what she wants to, even though I'm obviously avoiding the whole "ran into Joe" comment?

"She's really good. She keeps trying to hook me up with guys. I shouldn't expect any different, I guess."

I sigh in relief. "No, probably not. Something would be wrong if she wasn't trying to get you laid."

"I know, right?"

Margot is a year older than me. She was sick as a child and ended up having to repeat a year, which put her in my second grade class. We've been friends ever since. I've been working to get closer to her over the last few months, trying to let her in, to trust her and let her be more than just the good-time friend she's been in the past. Not by her doing, but mine. I've kept a part of myself locked away from her, from everyone.

Until Joseph, I never wanted to let anyone in, let them see all of me.

The good.

The bad.

The dark.

And the light.

Until him.

But it can't be him. For my own self-preservation, it cannot be Joseph. I need to move on like he so obviously has.

I continue to visit with Margot as I finish getting ready for work, and as I get in my car and drive to work. We talk about anything and everything, except Joseph. He's not open for discussion.

That doesn't exactly go toward my whole *letting-her-in* endeavor, but I can't talk about him. I'm trying the whole *he-doesn't-exist* tactic to see if my heart and my head will follow suit.

We hang up when I arrive. Work has been calm for the last few weeks, no more customers manhandling me. I get a little flirt now and then, but they're just being nice or trying to get a better place on the waiting list.

"Sam, that guy is back again." Becca tilts her chin to the bar.

I follow her line of sight. There's a guy who shows up a few nights a week, orders a drink or two and then leaves.

"Is it him? I can't tell from this angle." He's in a different seat than he normally sits in, but the bar is full for a Thursday night.

She rolls her eyes. "Seriously? It is so totally him. You need to tell Trent he's here again."

The guy's my dad's age. Trent and Becca say he stares at me when he's here, but I've never noticed. Every once in a while, I get a feeling like I'm being watched, but I can never nail him staring. A little staring seems harmless in comparison to the guy who grabbed me, so as long as this guy stays away, it's no big deal.

I hang out in the back during my break. Scott made me my favorite pasta dish. It's not even on the menu, or it's a combination of things on the menu he throws together to make improvised magic. He knows how much I like fettuccine alfredo, but it's too heavy and too many calories to eat very often so he lightens up the sauce and adds in lots of veggies with the grilled chicken or shrimp. Today it's big, plump shrimp.

"God, Scott, this is so good. Why is this not on the menu?" I don't understand it. There's gotta be people out there like me who want more than a light olive oil but less than an Alfredo sauce.

He chuckles. "You're easily pleased, Sam. Not everyone likes that mutt sauce with all those vegetables." He points to my bowl. "I think you're a rabbit with the amount of vegetables you like in your pasta."

"Oh man, the crisp veggies are the best part. And this shrimp too. You even pull the tails off for me so I don't have to get my fingers dirty."

He laughs again. "See, you're easily pleased."

"I just appreciate good food when I taste it." I glance at the clock. "Shit, I'm gonna be late." I hop off the table, and he takes the bowl.

"I'll put some in a to-go container for you and maybe your favorite cheesecake." He winks.

"Are you trying to fatten me up?" I don't need any help. I have enough curves at it is. I don't need any more.

"Sam, you enjoy your food. I'm a chef. We like feeding people who enjoy our cooking. It's ingrained in our blood or something."

I wipe my mouth and quickly put on lip gloss. "I'm glad me enjoying your food makes you happy. Because eating your food makes me happy. It's a win-win." I head for the door to relieve Becca.

"Sam." Scott's booming voice halts me before I reach the door. "Don't leave without me tonight. I heard that creep is out there again."

I roll my eyes. They're so overprotective since that guy grabbed me. I wish they'd relax. "I'll be fine." I turn to leave. "Besides, he's never even talked to me."

"Sam." His voice is firmer this time.

What is it with these dominant men and using their voices to impart their will?

"Yes?"

"I'll cut you off if you leave without me escorting you to your car. No more pasta. No more cheesecake. No more food of any kind."

"Well, now you're just being mean." I flip my hair as I spin around and exit the kitchen.

His deep laugh follows me as I walk away.

When it's time to leave, I don't wait for Scott. I clock out and slip out the door. I don't want to inconvenience Scott or anyone else by walking me to my car when they have better things to do. Besides, the guy they're concerned about left hours ago while I was on break.

I click the key fob to unlock my door. As my hand touches the door handle, the hairs on my neck stand on end.

"Sam," an unfamiliar voice calls from behind. I can't place his accent.

My hand stills for just a second too long when a hand touches my shoulder. I stiffen, but don't turn around. It feels safer to not turn around. To not see his face. But it also means I can't see to defend myself. I should have waited for Scott.

I square my shoulders as I slowly turn.

His hand drops, and he steps back.

That has to be a good sign. If he was going to hurt me he would have grabbed me quickly, taking me by surprise.

"You need to tell your father about me," he says matter-of-factly.

"What?" I step back, moving to put my car between us. "Who are you?"

He doesn't try to stop me. "Tell him you saw me," he says succinctly.

I shake my head. "I don't under—"

"Sam!" Bruce and Scott run toward me. *Thank fuck.*

"Get away from her, you motherfucker!" Scott bellows menacingly.

The man lumbers to a car parked an aisle over. "Tell him," he says again calmly. Too calmly. He doesn't seem concerned with Bruce or Scott rushing our way. He's not panicked. He moves like it was simply time for him to leave.

By the time Scott makes it to me, a few seconds before Bruce, the man has driven away. I slump against my car, bending forward, my hands on my knees. *Breathe.*

Tears prick my eyes as the weight of what just happened, what could have happened, crashes over me.

"Sam? You alright?" Scott's hands grasp me firmly, pulling me upright. "Shit. Don't cry." He pulls me into his tight embrace. "Did he touch you?"

I shake my head. "He just touched my shoulder. He didn't do anything."

"Why didn't you wait?" His voice is harsh, full of censure. Tears skate down my cheek, and he rubs my back. "Fuck, Sam. I'm sorry."

"I'm sorry. I really thought it was no big deal. Don't be mad." I couldn't stand it if these burly guys were mad at me. They're like big, protective teddy bears.

Bruce pipes in. "We're not mad, Sam. Just concerned. What if we hadn't shown up? What would have happened? Did you get his license plate?"

"No. I don't think he wanted to hurt me. He seems to know my father."

That gets their attention. I fill them in on all the guy said, which wasn't much.

I promise to not walk out by myself again, and convince them to let me drive home without an escort.

Scott kisses my cheek. "Don't scare me like that again." He chucks my chin. "Let me know when you get home safe."

"I will," I promise. "Thank you."

Scott squeezes my arm. "Anytime, Sam."

"Yeah, be safe getting home," Bruce chimes in.

I pull out, wiping at the tears starting to fall again as I turn away.

What did the stranger want?

What could have happened if they hadn't shown up?

The ache in my chest for Joseph grows stronger than ever before. All I want to do is climb onto his lap and find comfort in his warm embrace and gentle words.

Until I met him…I never wanted to find comfort outside of myself. I was strong and independent. Self-reliant.

Now I feel…

Unhinged.

Unmade.

Undone.

Maybe needing someone isn't such a bad thing, but needing someone who doesn't want you back is.

Thirteen

Joseph

I T'S ONLY A FEW DAYS TILL CHRISTMAS. IT'S BEEN A
month of hell. I've managed to keep my promise to myself not to call,
text, or email her, but the closer I get to her house, the harder my
heart argues with me.

Be with her.

Not now.

Those eyes.

No.

Those lips.

Man the fuck up.

Strawberry kisses.

No.

The feel of her in your arms.

Mine.

I'm hopeless. Fucking hopeless.

I pull into the driveway, picking up Jace at his parents' house. It's
cold for a Texas December. It feels like snow is coming. I slip on my
jacket as I trudge up the stairs and knock on the front door. I could have
met him at a bar, at my parents' place, at Fin's. I could have stayed in my
car and honked for him, but no, I'm here standing at Samantha's doorstep, picking up Jace, hoping I'll get a glimpse of her.

A sliver.

I'm a masochist.

Anything to hold me over. To either confirm she's nothing to me and I have simply canonized her memory, or to solidify she is, in fact, the goddess of my world.

There's mistletoe hanging above the door. My heart slams inside my chest. *Has Samantha kissed anyone under this mistletoe?*

The door swings open at the same time I hear the hum of the garage door opening.

"Joe, hi. Come in," Mrs. Cavanagh greets me with a huge smile and a kiss on my cheek.

"Hi, Mrs. Cavanagh. How are you?" I step inside.

"I'm good. It's great to see you. We've missed having you around since Thanksgiving."

"I've missed being here. It meant a lot to me to spend the week with y'all." The Cavanaghs have always been nice to me, but it was a great week, and not just because I spent so much time with Samantha. It was her family as a whole, making me feel welcome, a part of their family.

A flash outside catches my eye and I see Samantha driving off through the open front door.

Fuck.

She must have been the one who opened the garage a moment ago. It could be a coincidence, but I doubt it.

My stomach knots in the realization she doesn't want to see me.

Mrs. Cavanagh shuts the front door and continues to make small talk, unaware of the turmoil going on inside of me.

Jace trots down the stairs. "Hey, man." He's happy and oblivious as well.

"Hey." I nod, trying not to act like someone just shot my dog.

We say goodnight to Jace's mom and head out to my car.

"What's wrong with you, man?" he asks as I start the engine.

"Nothing." My irritation doesn't bode well for the evening's enjoyment.

I can feel his eyes on me, but he doesn't say anything, and I'm grateful for that at least.

"I need a drink. You good with driving home?" I don't plan on getting shit-faced, but I just might.

He glances at me, frowning. "Sure, man. You want to talk about what's crawled up your ass?"

"Nope."

"Okay."

Samantha

I can't believe I just snuck out of my own house. My stomach twists as the reality of my action settles. Did Joseph see me leave? What's he thinking? I drive through my neighborhood faster than I should, trying to expand the distance between us—and that of my dignity I've left behind.

It's Christmas break from school. I have to keep myself busy, and, most importantly, I need to stay away from him.

At the last minute, Jace told me Joseph was on his way over. I barely had any time to text Margot and make a dash for the garage as Joseph pulled up out front.

I suck.

I know.

It's not one of my most shining moments. But desperate times call for quick escapes.

Self-preservation.

Not seeing him or hearing from him has been like enduring the third level of hell. I've been doing better lately. Seeing him, hearing his voice, knowing he's right there in my home but not being able to be with him would be excruciating.

He's made it clear he doesn't want to pursue anything, so I'm not going to throw myself at him like a lovesick puppy, and if that means running away, then fine, I'm a coward.

I was actually looking forward to just relaxing at home and not having to be social. I guess I could have hidden in my room, but there was no guarantee I wouldn't see him. Maybe they were leaving right away, but I didn't have time to discuss the particulars of their plans before I made my impromptu escape.

Margot meets me in her driveway before I even pull to a stop.

I roll down my window as she nears. "Hey." My tone is apologetic for showing up like this.

"Hey." She bends down, leaning in my window. "I was thinking. Why don't we go to that place near the SMU campus we like? We can watch the college boys, get some good grub, listen to music…" She shrugs and gives me a soft smile. "…talk, if you want to. Or not. But, it'll be decidedly more fun than hanging out here." She wrinkles her nose and adds, "Dad's not in the best of moods. So, it's a win-win. We'll get to scope out hot college boys, and we don't have to listen to my dad whine about work, or the news, or my mom," she says the last part even more sadly.

Things must not be going well with her parents. They've had a rough couple of years, but it got worse when her dad lost his job last year. I don't really know all the details, but I know he's not happy with his current "temporary" job, as he refers to it.

I respond before I can overthink it. "Sounds like a great idea, actually." I motion to the passenger seat. "Hop in."

The place is packed, but we luck into a parking space near the entrance and snag a high table in the bar area just as another couple's leaving. It must be a sign we're supposed to be here.

My shoulders finally start to relax halfway through our burgers and a drawn out discussion on *Outlander* vs. *Game of Thrones*. I'm the *Outlander* fan, as it rocks, of course. She's *Game of Thrones* all the way.

We must have gotten too loud, too animated, as a sinfully sexy voice chimes in from behind me, "*Walking Dead.*"

Mid fry to my mouth, I stop and face that voice.

The guy it belongs to has beautiful blue eyes, highlighted by his tanned skin and black hair. Unusual features, delicate and yet masculine at the same time. Pretty. He's definitely a pretty boy, also tall, lean, and overly confident.

I cock a brow at him as he comes closer. "Excuse me?"

His devious smile crooks further. "*The Walking Dead.*"

He and his buddy come to stand next to our table. He sticks out his hand. "Sebastian." He motions to his friend. "Bobby."

So far, he's said seven words, none of them in complete sentences. His English teacher must be so proud right about now.

I take his hand firmly. No wussy handshakes here. "Sam," I simply reply before nodding across the table. "Margot."

"Pleasure," he says, meeting my eyes.

I can't help but laugh at his abbreviated speech. "Are you capable of speaking in complete sentences or are you going for the '*less is more*' approach?" I pull my hand out of his, seeing as how he doesn't seem inclined to release it on his own.

His head falls back, and a carefree laugh escapes his perfectly formed lips. Shaking his head, his eyes meet mine. "You're feisty, Sam. I like that."

He leans intimately closer and whispers, "I'm more than competent with my mouth, but wouldn't you feel bad if I were shy or had a speech impediment?"

I smirk. "Yes, actually I would. But, thankfully I don't have to apologize for being too candid."

"No, I suppose you don't. But you should probably apologize to the other women in this room."

He's lost me. "Why?"

"Because you're the most beautiful woman in here, and they don't stand a chance."

I scoff. "Seriously? Does that line actually work?"

"You tell me. I've never had a reason to use it before."

I almost buy it—he actually seems sincere. "Laying it on a little thick, don'tcha think?"

"I'm only calling it as I see it." His hand rests on the back of my chair as he snags a fry, giving me a devious smile and a raise of his eyebrow.

After a few more minutes of me rebuffing him, he dials down his charm a couple of decibels and ends up being a really nice guy. Margot and Bobby seem to be hitting it off, and the four of us delve into the topic that brought them to our table in the first place: the fact that Sebastian believes *The Walking Dead* is a far superior show to my *Outlander* chick-flick-kilt-wearing-time-period drama, or Margot's *Game of Thrones* kill-off-any-character-you-like-blood-bath-athon. In his humble opinion, of course.

"So, tell me, Sam. If I were to ask for your phone number, would you give it to me?" Hope glimmers in his eyes.

My heart pings for a man who's ever-present, yet strikingly absent from my life.

Sebastian is crazy good-looking and nice. I'm flattered, truly, but he's not Joseph.

I lower my gaze and my voice, hoping he hears my sincerity. "I'm not looking to get involved with anyone, Sebastian."

He nods in understanding. "I could use a friend. How about you?" His smile is sweet and genuine.

"They say you can never have too many friends."

His smile grows to show his perfectly straight white teeth. "Yes, *they* do say that." He places his phone in front of me. "Friends." He acquiesces to my limitation of our involvement.

I take his phone and wake up the screen, scold him for not having it password protected, then enter my number and name as *Sam My Super Cool Friend*. I then proceed to walk him through the steps to add a password to his phone.

He laughs. "You're such a dork."

I shake my head. "You have no idea how much of a dork I truly am."

We spend the next thirty minutes talking about the cell phone apps I've developed. He insists I pull them up so he can download them, paying for each without complaint. He even promises to recommend them to all his friends and family so they can do the same.

It's late by the time the four of us head out. The boys walk us to our car, pausing for a quick goodbye. I get a small hug and chaste kiss to my cheek. Margot gets a full kiss on the lips. I snicker when their kiss continues.

Sebastian nudges my shoulder. "Hey, I won over the prettiest girl in the room tonight. She even agreed to be my friend. I'd call it a stellar night."

I laugh and blush from the compliment.

We say goodnight again, and I slip into the driver's seat, starting my car, and wait for Margot to end her lip lock.

My phone dings with a text message from an unknown number: *Goodnight, beautiful Sam.*

I peer out my window and see Sebastian sitting a few cars over in a black sports car, waving at me.

I add him to my contacts and text back:

Me: *Goodnight, Sebastian of the Walking Dead.*

Sebastian: *LOL. Sweet dreams, Sam of Outlander.*

I turn my screen off, but continue to stare at it. I've gone years with no attention and now two of the hottest guys I've ever seen have given me the time of day. Joseph wanted me...at least enough to fool around with. Sebastian asked me out, but he's not Joseph.

Maybe I should give Sebastian a chance.

Maybe I could do casual.

Maybe if I see what else is out there, Joseph won't seem so perfect any more.

Fourteen

Joseph

CHRISTMAS AND NEW YEARS CREEP SLOWLY BY. I've been home for two weeks. Two long weeks of hanging out with my parents, brothers, and friends. No women. None. I can't have the only woman I want, and she haunts my days and my nights. I've been to Jace's four times and each time Samantha wasn't there.

Jace, of course, is being Jace, and giving me shit about pining over his kid sister. He's uncharacteristically harsh about it even though I told him I'd keep my distance from her. I'm not exactly sure what's bugging him: the fact I'm attracted to his sister, or me being a baby about it.

"You're such a pussy," he says as we step off the elevator, having arrived at Fin's penthouse aloft MCI Towers.

I halt in my tracks, making him stop to avoid running into my back, and pivot to face him.

"Why exactly is that, Jace?" I grab the back of my neck and squeeze to alleviate the tension building there. "Because I care for your sister? Because I respect her enough not to lead her on, making promises I'm in no position to fulfill?" I step closer, towering over him. "Would you rather I fuck her and leave her?"

He steps back, appalled. "Jesus, no."

I press forward. "Am I a pussy because I prefer not to fuck every skirt that looks my way in an effort to forget her?"

"No," he says solemnly.

"So, I'm a pussy because I physically ache for her, like I left a part of me behind the day we left your house after Thanksgiving break?"

"No." His eyes slowly rise to mine. "Well, maybe. You're just not yourself. It's like you can't function without her," he says in disbelief, unable to fathom what that would even be like.

I sigh and step back. "You're right. I'm not myself. And I'm pissed about it. I'm distracted, unfocused." I sigh and pin him with my gaze. "I feel undone, incomplete, with no end in sight."

"Yeah, like a pussy," Jace says again, only laughing this time.

I chuckle, feeling some of the tension leave my body. "Don't let Samantha hear you say that. She'd be offended you're using a reference to the female anatomy with a derogatory connotation."

"No shit," he agrees.

Most women would find it offensive. I'm disheartened we continually use terms related to women as derogatory putdowns toward men.

Fin opens his front door. "You pussies gonna come in or stay out in the hall gabbing like a bunch of women?"

Jace and I bust out laughing. I can't even catch my breath to explain why as I walk past Fin.

We're greeted by my brother Matt, who shakes our hands as our laughter wanes and we compose ourselves.

"Hey, Joe." Victor greets me with a smile and a pat on the back. He's MCI's head of security, who doubles as Fin's driver much of the time.

"Hey, man." I return his pat as he shakes hands with Jace.

A familiar face turns the corner. I grin. "Michael, it's been ages. How are you?"

"I'm good. I hear you're hung up on Jace's sister." He graces me with a rare smile.

I just shrug and head to the kitchen for a much-needed beer. The guys follow, picking up the drinks they left behind to meet us at the door.

Fin stands next to me. "I was getting ready to open the door when

I saw you turn and nearly pounce on Jace. Was that about Sam?" He keeps his voice low so only I can hear.

I keep mine equally low to be sure Jace can't hear me. "Yeah, he called me a pussy, and I lost it for a minute." I take a pull of my beer. "We're good now."

"Hmm, but you're not really good, are you?" He's perceptive as ever.

I exhale. "Let's just play some poker and give me something else to focus on, yeah?"

He squeezes my shoulder. "You got it." He eyes my beer. "If you need to stay the night, you know my door is always open."

I nod, grateful. "Thanks, brother, but I'm done drowning my sorrow."

"Fair enough." He turns to razz the other guys in the group. "Should we get this game started? Or do you just want to hand over your money now?"

"In your dreams," Matt replies.

"Not happening, asshole," Victor pushes back.

He and Fin have a tight bond that goes beyond boss and employee. They met in high school. Victor's a few years older, but they remained in contact as Fin went to college and Victor went into the military—where he met Michael—and then did a stint in the FBI. Michael and Victor have become a part of our tight-knit group, *The Six Pack* as my father dubbed us when Jace joined a few years ago. Jace is the latest member, but you'd never think he wasn't one of us all along.

As Fin and Matt's younger brother, I was included even though I was entirely too young for most of their antics, but they looked out for me, kept me clean and out of trouble. Though, I did get more than a few beers before I was of legal age. Like tonight, Jace gets two beers, no more. Fin is a stickler for that rule. If anyone has more than two drinks, they stay the night, no discussion. Fin isn't as tall as me, or as thick, but he's strong as shit with a menacing glare that brooks no arguments from anyone. Not even Victor and Michael with their military backgrounds push Fin. He's calm, cool, and collected 99% of the time, but it's that 1% that makes grown men quake in their shoes.

With boastful pride, we take our seats as Fin exchanges our money for chips.

"So, Fin, you getting any, or are you still hanging onto your virginity for dear life?" Michael locks eyes with Fin.

"Fuck off, Michael. You know your mother was my first."

The four of us not in this conversation bust out laughing.

The gleam in Fin's eyes tells me he's not done. "But you were my second, Michael. And to be honest, I'm not sure who was the better fuck." Fin doesn't skip a beat as he deals the cards.

"Fuck, Fin," Michael exclaims. "You had to go there, always have to one-up me." He takes a long drink of his beer. "Jesus, those are two images I'll never get out of my head now. Thanks, man."

"Anytime, lover." Fin winks at Michael.

"Knock it the fuck off, Fin." Michael stalks to the kitchen and comes back with six shot glasses and bottle of Crystal Skull Vodka.

Shit. Fin was just kidding, but Michael's a hard ass of the highest degree. Kidding around about his sexuality is not something he takes lightly. I glance at Fin to get his beat on the situation.

"Michael, man," Fin says softly. "You know I'm just kidding, right?"

Michael pours a shot and throws it back before responding. "Yeah. I know."

"Besides. You're the best fuck I've ever had," Fin throws out with all sincerity before he winks. "Here, let me get you another one." He pours Michael another shot.

Michael throws it back muttering, "Fuckface."

Fin takes a shot himself, then prompts our big and small blinds. "Ante up, boys. It's time for this *'fuckface'* to take your money."

The laughter slowly dies down. The shots of vodka continue, and even Jace partakes, which means he's staying over. I resist the hard stuff and switch to soda after my first beer. I've had enough of drinking for a while. I'm done trying to lose myself in a bottle to avoid thinking of Samantha.

We stick to Texas Hold'em for the next hour or so. It's a serious but friendly game, meaning we play by the rules, but we still give each other shit.

I'm up a hundred bucks, which is impressive with these guys. It's not like playing a bunch of college boys. These are some seriously talented players.

Just to goad me, Michael tries to distract me with questions about Samantha.

By the third one, Jace has had enough. "God, can we not talk about Sam tonight? Please," he grumbles from across the table. He keeps his eyes on his cards before he sets them face down and raises Victor. His glare narrows on me. "Besides, man, she's on a date tonight. You need to get over it."

I slump back in my chair as if he physically slapped me, though it feels more like a punch in the gut.

Goddammit.

"Jace," Fin barks at him.

Before they can get into it. I stand up, throwing my cards on the table. "Fold."

I scrub my face with my hands, stumbling back. *Fuck.* I'm going to be sick, physically sick. "Deal me out," I mutter as I head to the living room, but I don't stop until I make it to the nearest bathroom.

I splash cold water on my face, leaning against the counter.

I've lost her. She's moving on.

My gut revolts, saliva coating my mouth. I swallow hard, breathe deep, and rinse my mouth with water from the tap, hoping it will help. I didn't want to tie her down before she got to experience more, but I didn't expect it to feel this awful.

"I can't lose her," I mutter, standing to dry my face and hands.

A knock at the door startles me. "Joe, you okay, man?"

"I need a minute, Fin."

I need more than a minute. I need two-and-a-half years to have passed so Samantha has graduated early from college. I'll have graduated and settled into my job. She'll be twenty, and I'll be twenty-three, both more mature with our futures in hand. There'll be nothing to keep me from pursuing her.

But fuck, that's not the case. The reality of waiting all that time to be with her falls on my shoulders like a lead vest. Who's to say she won't fall in love with this asshole and forget all about me?

Of course she's not going to fucking wait on me. I never asked her to wait, but I'd hoped that she would.

Mine.

The thought creeps in and won't leave, tightening like a vise around my chest.

Mine.

I pull my phone out and dial her number before I can stop myself. As it rings, I lean back against the counter.

"Hello?" Her voice is uncertain. It's taken balls of steel not to call her every fucking day even though I've had her number all this time.

My dick goes hard from the simple sound of her voice. "Sweetness," I croak out.

"Joseph?"

I hear so much in that one word. Surprise. Hope. *Mine.*

"Are you alright? You don't sound alright. What's wrong?" Her voice jumps up in volume as her concern escalates.

"Where are you?" I don't have time for small talk, and I'm most definitely not alright. There's noise in the background and a man's voice.

"I…um…I'm out."

"Where are you?" I ask more firmly.

"Houston's." She pauses then adds, "What's wrong?" Her voice is soft, her concern apparent.

Despite my absence, her efforts to avoid me, and the fact that she's out with another guy, she still cares.

My heart pounds in my ears. "I just…need to see you." I ache for more, but it's a start.

"Now's not a good time. I can call you later."

Later? Well, at least she didn't say never.

"Promise?"

"Yes, I promise. I'll call you back in a few hours. When I get home."

I take a deep breath and let it out. "Okay. Later, then."

"Okay." Her relief is apparent.

"Samantha?"

"Yes?"

Don't move on without me. I don't say what I want to and struggle to find something of importance that won't freak her out. "Be safe," I eventually say. *That was lame.*

"Safe?" she questions.

"Yeah, don't do anything…foolish."

She giggles. She must think I'm ridiculous. "Okay. I'll stay safe and won't do anything foolish. I promise." She covers her phone and then comes back. "I have to go. Our food just arrived."

Fuck. *Their* food.

"You'll call?" I press.

"Yes, I said I would." She reassures, not scolds. "Goodbye, Joseph."

"Till later, Sweetness…never goodbye."

Her breath catches.

Fuck. She likes what I just said.

"Later, then."

Her words hang in my head as I pace the bathroom a few times.

I make a decision, probably rash, but one I will in no way regret.

I glance in the mirror. Finding myself acceptable, I shrug and open the bathroom door. I can hear the guys continuing their poker game in the dining room as I slip out the front door and send Fin a quick text:

Me: *I'm heading out.*

Fin: *U OK?*

Me: *I gotta go see about a girl.*

Fin: *Pussy.*

Me: *Yep, but only for her.*

Samantha

I hang up, take a calming breath, set my phone in my purse, and sheepishly meet Sebastian's gaze. "I'm sorry about that."

He agreed this wasn't a date, but it was still rude to answer my phone. I normally wouldn't have, especially for an unknown number, but I felt like I needed to answer it.

I'm glad I did.

It was good to hear Joseph's voice, but he didn't sound quite right.

Sebastian smiles. "Was it him? The one who's locked down your heart?"

Has he? "Yes and no. It's not like that. We're not together. We're... not in love."

He nods as he forks a bite of food. "Yeah, I gathered as much from what you've said so far." He points at me. "And the sadness on your face when you think of him."

I guess I'm no good at hiding my misery.

We sit in silence for a few minutes as we eat, him more enthusiastically than me. I've lost my appetite. This is my favorite place, and I'm letting Joseph ruin my dinner with Sebastian. It doesn't matter why Joseph called—he and I are never going to be together.

I try to get Sebastian and me back on track. "So, Dr. Cole, tell me what it's like to be a Resident in the ER."

He narrows his eyes at me and frowns. "No." He dismisses my question, setting down his fork. "What's the deal anyway? Why can't you be together? Is he an ass or something?"

I push my food around my plate. "No, he's not an ass. It's just...we need to focus on graduating and our careers, and not get into a relationship." I lean back and take a long drink of iced tea. "Neither of us wants or needs the distraction. Plus..." I look away, not wanting to finish that thought.

"Plus what? He's an ass? See, I knew it," Sebastian jokes.

I laugh. "No, he's not an ass." Wiping my mouth, I set down my napkin and lean forward. "It's just who he is, or rather who he's going to be. He needs someone else...not...me," I huff.

"He said that?"

I shake my head. "He didn't need to say it. So...what's the point?"

"Let me get this straight. This guy you're longing for, missing, you don't see a future with, and yet, you're holding out for him. Not dating anyone else, for what? Forever?"

"I'm not trying to wait for him." I shake my head. "It sounds stupid, I know. But just because the timing isn't right for us now, doesn't mean I don't want it *now*. And just because he doesn't see me with him for the long haul, doesn't mean I don't want it all the same."

"That's so sad, Sam."

I nod and have to bite my lip to keep from crying. "It is. It truly is."

He studies me for a few minutes as I pick at my food.

"You're beautiful. Too beautiful and nice to spend your youth pining for some guy." He waves his hand in dismissal. "You shouldn't be alone." He leans forward. "And you're miserable."

I force a smile and nearly choke on my words. "I'm not miserable."

He lets out a small chuckle. "Ah, Sam. You are, baby." He lays his hand over mine and squeezes. "You don't have to be, though. Spend time with me. I'll help you forget. Help you get over him."

I pull my hand away. What he says is sweet and kind, and may be just a ploy to get in my pants, but he seems to honestly care. Still, I don't want to give Sebastian the wrong idea. "That's just it. I don't *want* to forget him."

The back of my neck prickles, and I feel that familiar buzz in the air. My breath catches when I see Joseph approaching our table.

"Samantha," he says simply, but there is nothing simple about the need in his voice or the heat in his eyes.

"Joseph." I'm surprised he's here, and yet I'm not. He said he needed to see me and sounded desperate on the phone.

His greedy eyes pin me to my seat before slipping across the table to Sebastian. A curt nod is all the greeting Sebastian gets. "Could I speak to you for a moment?" Joseph holds out his hand.

"I..." I peel my eyes off Joseph. Sebastian eyes are wide, his lips tight. "I'll be back."

I don't wait for his reply before I take Joseph's hand and slip out of the booth.

Joseph laces his fingers through mine and pulls me past the bar and kitchen, dodging staff and patrons as we go. I thought he would head outside, but there's a dark alcove between the men's and women's restrooms. He stops there and whips me around so I'm flush against the wall near the corner.

My breath catches. "What are you doing here?"

He moves in, hovering over me. One hand rests against the wall above my head, and the other is clutching my waist, pressing me to him, holding me tightly, protecting me from prying eyes. His head lowers to mine. "Sweetness," he breathes out before his lips crash into mine.

My entire body comes alive as he presses forward, pinning me against the wall. His arms, wrapped around me, hold me as if he can't get me close enough.

He groans into my mouth when my hands move along his body, holding him just as tight so he can't escape. I don't want him to let me go. Ever.

I'd not forgotten the taste of him, the smell of him, but I'm still overwhelmed. It all comes flooding back. His kiss softens as his tongue plunges deep and undoes all my work to forget him over the last few weeks. I pour all my pent-up frustration and desire for this man into kissing him back.

That small tender reprieve ends the moment his erection presses into me and I moan. He doesn't let up. Instead he ratchets up the tension when he moves between my legs. My flowy skirt gives him all the access he needs to press his jean-clad thigh between mine. His urgent, possessive kisses return as he swallows every bit of passion I have to give, his hand squeezing my ass, grinding me against him.

I gasp as he hits that spot, and it only fuels the fire.

He groans, his need as apparent as mine. He rocks me against him again and again as his mouth devours me.

My fingers dig into the taut, strained muscles of his back as I begin to tremble, reaching for release. The tingle starts in my legs, working its way up, growing like a bubble as it moves up my body, consuming me, rising higher and higher, expanding, until the tension is so tight it can't grow any more.

"That's it, Sweetness," he says a second before my orgasm bursts forth like fireworks, and I cry out as I come. Joseph swallows the sound, supporting me as I quake in his arms.

His kisses soften and move to my face, my jaw, and my neck.

He nuzzles into my hair, his breathing strained, his heart pounding in his chest, matching mine. "Don't go out with anyone else," he whispers in my ear. "Wait for me, Samantha."

My insides clench, sending another wave of shudders through my body.

"That's right, beautiful. Give me every bit of your pleasure."

He pulls a chair sitting only a few feet away over to our darkened corner and sits down, cradling me in his lap, my head buried in his neck. We're tight in each other's embrace.

"Only me." His voice is strained. "Don't give yourself to him or anyone else." He cradles my cheek. "I don't deserve you. But please, Samantha, wait for me. Please."

His pleas rip a hole in the wall I've put around my fears, my desires, my hopes surrounding him. The tears start to fall, as much as I try to hold them back. He didn't call or text or talk to me for over a month until he found out I was on a date. He doesn't want me—or does he? He's here right now...surely that means something, but I can't think with what he did to my body a moment ago.

"Shh. Don't cry," he coos into my hair and continues to comfort me as I recover from my orgasm and the emotional turmoil that is Joseph McIntyre.

I'm sure I'll be embarrassed later for what's happening right here near the restrooms, but at this moment, I feel cocooned and safe in his arms.

"You're so sexy, Samantha. That was hot as fuck." His smile warms me.

I'm so confused. "Why are you here? You made it clear you don't want a relationship with me. You never called or anything, but you want me to ignore Sebastian? You can't have it both ways."

He holds me tightly as he gently wipes my tears away. "Just because I didn't call doesn't mean I wasn't thinking of you every day. I need time to figure things out. Can you give me that?"

Can I? I touch his face, peering into his worried eyes. "Sebastian and I are just friends."

He searches my face for confirmation of my words, then nods, pulling me closer, burying his head in my neck. "My girl," he whispers.

My heart aches as his words echo in my head. I am his girl even though I tried not to be.

Once composed, I slip into the restroom to freshen up and gain some perspective.

I head to the nearest stall. I can't believe I just made out—and had an orgasm in public. Granted it was a secluded corner, but anyone could have walked by and witnessed my undoing. Luckily, that didn't happen.

He came here for me. Why?

I don't trust that I'll remember what it felt like to be in his arms hours from now. I close my eyes and relive every second, focusing on his touch and his words.

Time. He asked for time.

When I exit the restroom, I'm disappointed that Joseph isn't there waiting for me.

Maybe he's in the men's room. I wait for a few minutes, then decide I should get back to the table. What will I say to Sebastian? Some form of the truth, but most definitely not all of the truth.

I stop in my tracks when I see Joseph sitting in my spot, talking to

Sebastian. Their conversation is intense, their expressions serious and locked in on each other. Joseph is talking and Sebastian is nodding. I can't make out any words, but it's obvious Joseph is laying something out, and Sebastian is in agreement.

With a final nod, Joseph stands, shaking Sebastian's hand. He turns and walks toward me, as if he knew I was here the entire time. Maybe he can sense me too.

He pulls me into his arms and kisses me tenderly, his tongue just barely brushing my lips. "You're mine."

He starts to pull away, but I grab his shirt and pull him back, kissing him fiercely. His hands grip my sides, tightening their hold as he kisses me back.

When I pull away, I say quietly, but firmly. "I'm not yours. I'm nobody's."

His dimpled smile weakens my knees. "You aren't nobody's." He kisses me one more time and steps back. "I just need time." He winks at me as he releases his hold and slips out of the busy restaurant.

I watch until he is out of sight and then join Sebastian.

"You alright? You're flushed," Sebastian says once I'm settled on my side of the booth. My seat is still warm from Joseph.

"Yes, I'm fine." I take a bite of my grilled chicken salad with renewed hunger. Even though I'm more confused than ever, I feel better for having seen Joseph. Knowing that our attraction is still mutual. Real. He said he thought of me every day. I feel a sense of power that I didn't feel before. He's jealous—crazed by the idea of me being with someone else. We may not be together, but we're not with anyone else either. And that's something.

Is it enough? No. Though at the moment I'm high on endorphins and quite elated that he came after me and claimed me so intimately and publicly for anyone to have seen. I want to call Margot and scream over the phone that Joseph gave me my first orgasm. Well, first orgasm by someone other than myself. He asked for time. Does that mean he wants to be together? He wouldn't ask me to wait forever…

I don't want to analyze the shit of this. Not yet, anyway. I just want to bask in the glow of his touch, his desire for *me*. His jealousy over *me* being out with another guy. I've never felt so wanted, and I try to hold on to that feeling for as long as I can before my natural inclination to logically dismiss it all overrules my euphoric state.

PART 6
FAMILY TIES

FEBRUARY

Fifteen

Samantha

MOM AND DAD ARE LEAVING FOR VACATION today, and I'm in the driveway helping my dad load their luggage in the car. Mom packs like they'll be gone for a month instead of seven days. Dad doesn't complain, though; that's just Mom. He says packing heavy helps her relax and feel prepared, and he would rather she be relaxed than fight about the contents of her suitcase.

My dad's a wise man. He dotes on Mom and loves her more than I've ever seen a man love a woman. He doesn't sweat the small stuff. He gives her the freedom to be who she is and indulges her idiosyncrasies. She does the same, but he doesn't seem to have many.

This isn't the first time they've left me alone since Jace has been at college, but it's the longest time they'll have been away. I'm fine with it. Spring Break is in a month, and I have a project due before then. I'll spend my time focusing on that.

Mom finally makes it outside after checking and double-checking she has everything. She gives me a big hug. "Be good. Have fun but not too much fun." She kisses my cheek and moves to the passenger door where she stops and faces me. "I know you will, but I have to say it for my own peace of mind. Be responsible. No boys. No parties." She lets out a deep breath, and her shoulders relax now that she's said her piece.

I laugh. She's nervous. "Mom, I know the rules. I'm too busy for parties and boys, anyway."

Besides, there is only one man I want, and he's four hours away at college, living with my brother. Probably dating girls his own age. No, not girls. Women.

Shit. I had to go there.

Joseph said he's not interested in dating anyone else, but still, he's twenty-one and a sexual male. I don't expect him to go without. There might not be *dating*, but I don't imagine his bed is empty either.

I shake my head, trying to dismiss those thoughts.

Dad lays a kiss on my cheek. "She's just nervous about leaving you for a whole week. We trust you, Sam." He gives me a quick hug. "Don't disappoint us."

There it is. He had to get in his parental gibe as well.

"Geez, you two, I got this. I'm not gonna have a party, go to a party, have boys over, drink, or have sex. I'm going to attend school, work, hang with Margot, and maybe Sebastian, but mostly, it'll just be about school and work." As usual.

Feeling satisfied with that answer, Dad turns to Mom. "Come on, gorgeous, we've got a plane to catch and a bikini for me to get you out of."

OMG! I groan.

"I heard that, Sam. I'm a man. I still love your mother. Get over it." He winks at me. "Love you, pumpkin. Call if you need us."

With a final wave, they back out of the driveway and head to the airport.

I'm not even fifteen minutes into my solitude when I get a text from Jace.

Jace: *Freedom! Whatcha gonna do with it?*

Me: *Have an orgy and burn the house down around me, of course!*

Jace: *Ah, that's my girl. I've taught you well.*

My cell phone rings. "What, you can't stand that you might be missing out on the fun?" I tease.

"Well, hello to you too, sis." Jace chuckles. "I figured I could call you instead of texting."

"I'm sorry. Hello, dearest brother, how are you?"

"Alright, smartass. Enough of that." There's muffled discussion in the background, then his voice is back. "Sorry about that. Joe says *hi.*"

I laugh even though my insides ache at hearing his name. "And you seem overjoyed to be telling me."

He sighs heavily. "Look, I don't know what went on with the two of you, and I prefer not to know, but he's been a miserable ass since Christmas." He huffs. "Actually, I take that back. He's been a miserable ass since he met you at Thanksgiving. Maybe you two should talk."

My head swims with too many ways to respond. I'm both happy and sad that Joseph is in knots just as much as I am. "He's not asking to talk to me, is he?"

It's been radio silence for two months now. No contact at all. The incident at the restaurant feels like a perfect, weird hallucination. I thought he'd change, start calling or something after claiming me as his in that way…but nothing happened. He wants me to wait for him, but then doesn't freaking talk to me. It's like he wants me to be miserable. I don't get it, and maybe I don't care to. "He could have called if he wanted to talk to me."

"No, that's my suggestion. But it's obvious to me that you want to talk to each other."

"There's no point, Jace. He doesn't like me like that."

"I don't think that's true, not by how he's acting."

"When have you known him to not pursue something he really wanted?"

Jace sighs. "Never. He's the most determined guy I know."

"Exactly." My throat burns at the truth Jace just admitted. "If he wanted to be with me, he would."

"You could talk as friends."

"No." I have to take a few deep breaths before I can continue. "Tell him I said *hi.*"

He sighs again before he continues, "Just so you know, he's not dating or anything. There's no women."

"That should make me happy, but it doesn't. Even though he doesn't want me enough, I don't want him to be alone. He's too great of a guy." I wipe a tear away and try to curb the emotion in my voice. "I can't do this with you, Jace. I appreciate your concern, but we can't talk about this anymore. I don't want to know if he's dating anyone or even if he's not. Because one of these days, you're not going to tell me he's not seeing anyone, which will mean he is, and it'll break my heart."

Fuck. Stop crying, right now!

"Please don't cry, Sam." He lets out a long breath. "I hate this."

"Yeah, well, it is what it is. So, listen, I've got this crack-pipe calling my name and that orgy to get to, so if there's not some more heartbreaking stuff you'd like to discuss, I've gotta hop on that dick waiting for me."

"Jesus, Sam. That's not even funny." I can practically see him grimace.

"Yeah, it is. Just a little." I laugh as tears fall, and I cover my mouth to stop a sob from escaping.

I hate this. I hate this so much. Why can't I tell him how much it hurts? Why do I have to pretend I'm okay, when clearly I'm not?

"Okay, maybe just a little, because it's not true. But don't talk like that. It's so raunchy. I understand you're just trying to lighten your mood and stop your girly emotions, but you don't have to drum up degrading images to do it."

I take a deep breath and clench my fist, digging my nails into my palm. "Desperate times call for desperate measures. Anyway, tell me what you're doing today."

"I've got homework, and then tending bar later this afternoon. If I didn't have such a busy schedule, I'd come home and spend the weekend with you."

"It's okay. I've got a lot of homework to do, and then work tonight."

In a quick rush of words, he apologizes for what happened when he was home for Thanksgiving. He also shares the news of the ban he and his friends put out on me when I was fourteen and reinforced at every turn. It actually makes me feel good. I'm sure he thought I would be upset with him, but, I said, "Honestly, it probably was a good thing."

"Yeah?" he asks, surprised.

"It allowed me to keep my focus on my education instead of being sidetracked by boys and all the messy stuff that comes with teen love and heartache."

Kinda like what you're going through now?

"I also told Veronica to go take a flying leap and never darken my or your doorstep again."

I'm sure his actual words were much more colorful and less diplomatic. I wish I could have heard it. "Really?"

"Joseph went with me for backup, just in case I fell prey to her wanton ways. I ended up doing just fine."

"I can't believe you did that for me."

"I love you, Sam. You're the best person I know. I want to be just like you when I grow up."

"Shit, Jace. Are you trying to make me cry again?"

He laughs. "No. But I have to say this, and then we won't talk about it again, at least not until the timing is better. Joe is the second-best person I know, and if you two can make it work, I'm behind you 110%. Anything you need, I'm there for you, even if it means not talking about the elephant in the room."

"I love you, Jace. I'd do anything for you too. You know that, right?"

"Well, what's not to love?" he jokes.

I'm thankful for him turning the heavy back into light again. "Exactly. Okay, go rock your life, kick ass, and take names."

"You too. Bye, sis."

"Bye, bro."

An hour later I get a text:

Joseph: *Sweetness, I heard you were crying today. I'm sorry I'm not the one to dry your tears. I'm YOURS. There's no one else. No women. No one but you. Remember that. We just need time.*

Time.

I plop down on my bed, trying to think of a response. A million things run through my mind, but none of them are appropriate for the type of relationship we're trying to maintain. All of them tell him how much I miss him. How much I hate the distance between us, both physically and emotionally. All of them open my heart up even more to the brokenness I fear is inevitable.

I need to stay focused on school and not get sidetracked with the what-ifs. The bottom line is these are just words, and his actions say he doesn't want me as I am today, not enough to fight for it. Who's to say he'll want me enough in the future? How much time does he want and to what end? And why the hell won't he even talk to me if I'm supposed to be waiting for him?

Before I can come to any conclusion on what to say back, my phone chimes with another text.

Joseph: *Tell me you hear me.*
Me: *I hear you. You're saying you're MINE.*
Joseph: *Yes. And YOU. ARE. MINE.*

His. But not in any tangible way. Not in a way that soothes my ache and comforts my thoughts.

Words.

All he's given me are more words. A throwaway text after two months of nothing.

Easily broken.

Easily forgotten.

Easily left behind.

Joseph

Dad and my brothers are flying in to have a family meeting with me. I'm concerned. They've never done this before, and I'm wondering what's so urgent it couldn't wait until I'm home for spring break next month. Dad insisted taking a few hours out of his Saturday to fly in was no hardship, and I haven't been home since New Years, so it'll be good to see them, but I'm worried all the same.

Jace is at the library studying and then works tonight. I have the house to myself and have been anxious since Jace's phone call with Samantha this morning. I tried not to listen, but when I heard him tell her not to cry, my resolve broke, as did my heart. The idea of her being alone in that big house crying nearly had me driving to Dallas to be sure she's okay. If my family wasn't flying here, I would have already driven there and had her in my arms by now. I'm so close to breaking all my plans, just to be near her.

I'm trying to be mature by staying away from her, but it's never been more difficult than it was this morning. I felt a modicum of peace after texting with her. She was reserved in her words, but I believe she's just trying to protect her heart. I don't blame her. I'm trying to protect her heart too. I'd do anything for her, and if it means staying away from her and reducing contact as much as possible, then that's what I'll do.

I screwed up that night at the restaurant, but the thought of her on a date with someone else…I had to see her, damn the consequences. And the memory of the way she looked, smelled, the sounds she made when I made her come…it's enough to keep me going.

It shouldn't have happened, and I shouldn't have slipped and told her to wait for me. It's obviously made things harder, more confusing for her. But if she knew the timeline, it would basically press pause on her life.

My career is important, my family is important. I'm not sure I can say they are more important to me than her anymore. My own happiness is not more important than hers. She needs time to find out who she is, live her life, and finish college. She needs to be sure I'm the one for her, because once I decide to go for it, once I have her—nothing's going to stand in my way.

But it's taken everything I have in me not to break down and call her every fucking day.

A sharp knock at my door alerts me to my family's arrival.

I swing open the door, happy for the interruption of my pondering and the familiarity of my dad and brothers.

"Hey, Dad." I give him a hug as he walks in.

"It's good to see you, son." He pats me hard on the back and moves on to the living room.

"Hey." Matt gives me a big hug. He's a hugger, gets it from our mom. He has a soft heart like her too, though he does a good job of hiding it.

"Good to see you," I say after he releases me.

Fin steps in last, giving me a hug and a manly kiss on the cheek. He's always been affectionate with me, maybe more so than with Matt. He doesn't judge me for my feelings for Samantha. He's supportive, though I don't think he truly understands the depths of my feelings.

"Brother," he says.

"Fin," I reply, getting the distinct feeling I'm not going to like this visit much.

He nods as if to confirm my suspicions.

I follow them into the living room, my heart pounding. It feels like the time I snuck out of the house and took Mom's car. I lost my virginity that night. Managed to make it home without anyone finding out, or so I thought. Dad cornered me in the kitchen the next day insisting I tell him where I'd gone and what I'd done. The high from experiencing sex for the first time came crashing down with Dad's reprimand. Matt sat at the kitchen table snickering over his bowl of cereal. Fin called me later, from college, to congratulate me on getting grounded and laid all in one fell swoop.

I told him it was totally worth it.

I wonder if my argument today will be the same.

More as a delay tactic than being a good host, I ask if they'd like anything to drink or eat.

"Joe. Sit." My dad is a man of few words. He believes in direct communicating with no frills to distract from the message.

I sit in the only remaining chair, waiting for what I'm positive is going to be an unpleasant conversation.

After a few moments of blaring silence and pointed glances between me and my brothers, I break. "What's going on, Dad?"

He clears his throat, something he always does before he dons his *boardroom* voice. My brothers and I were too young to know what he really sounded like in the boardroom, but it was something our grandfather had said one time and it stuck. Whenever it was discipline time, Dad brought out the boardroom voice, and we knew shit was getting serious.

"How are you doing?" Dad asks, not using his boardroom voice at all.

I'm shocked and thrown off now, unsure what to expect. "I'm fine."

He nods slowly, understanding *fine* is not at all how I am.

"How's Sam?" He surprises me again.

He's showing me his hand, going about it gently instead of power-housing me. But either way, if he wants to talk about my relationship with Samantha, this is not going to go well. I crack my neck and stand up. I'm taller than all of them, particularly my dad, who's closer to Jace's height at six-two. I may not have the financial or business backbone he has, but I have my height and pure determination to not let him or anyone else intimidate me.

I take a step closer to him, not hiding my distrust of this line of questioning. "Why do you ask?"

He chuckles and sits back in the chair with the air of a man who doesn't have a worry in the world. "It's a simple question, son. It should have a simple answer."

"She's fine," I bark.

He laughs again, and it pisses me off. I glance at Fin and Matt, who both look like they'd rather be anywhere else but here right now.

"What's this about?" I'm not one to beat around the bush either.

"I'm concerned for your future. Your determination to focus on your career, to focus on MCI." There, he finally got to the point.

"Nothing has changed, Dad. I'll graduate next year and then head up the tech side of MCI," I say flatly. "I've stayed in contact with Uncle Max, as usual." Well, maybe I haven't been *exactly* as on top of things—I drank heavily for a while after Thanksgiving trying to forget her, but I'm back on track. "Nothing's changed," I reiterate.

He leans forward. "*Nothing* has changed?" His eyebrows nearly disappear under the sweep of hair on his forehead.

"No." I try to steel my words with the conviction I'm not necessarily feeling.

"Son, I recognize a man in love when I see one. And you're sick as a dog who got hold of a rat poison-laced bone. You can't see straight. You're not eating properly, and you can't concentrate for shit. She's got you all tied up in knots inside and out." He stands and moves to me, placing his hand firmly on my shoulder. "Have I missed anything?"

I slump, the air in my sails deflated. "No, that pretty much sums it up."

He smiles and pulls me into an unexpected hug. "Love is the greatest gift you'll ever receive, until it's not. It can rot your brain if you let it." He pulls back, placing both hands on my shoulders, holding me at arm's length. "This can go one of two ways, son. You let your love for this woman make you stronger and more determined than ever to reach your goals, so you can be the man you are destined to be and the man she deserves. Or, you let this love sidetrack you, turn your brain to mush, and sour your future and hers." He releases me and returns to his chair. "You've moped around long enough over your situation. You need to take the bull by the horns and show it who's in control."

I sit down, stunned by his words. "You're not telling me to forget her?"

His face softens with a warm smile. "Joe, she's a wonderful girl. She's bright, determined, comes from a good family, and she's already a part of the MCI family. She wants a future there. You want a future there. You like each other—maybe even love each other. I have no doubt you two will make a powerful team, if you can just get out of your way long enough to focus on what needs to happen to make a successful run at it."

"You like her?" I'm still surprised by his support. I thought for sure he'd tell me my life has no room for love right now.

He chuckles and points to Fin and Matt sitting like bumps on a log. "You're the youngest, but maybe the brightest of your brothers. You've already figured out there's more to life than a successful career. It took me a while to figure it out, but your mother is the best thing that ever happened to me. *She* gives my life meaning. And you boys." He shakes his head at Matt, who's pulled out his phone and tuned us all out. "To answer your question, yes, Joseph, I like her a lot. I can't wait to welcome her into our family. *After* you two graduate from college." He leans forward. "Stick to the plan, son. Find a way you two can coexist and still function to make that happen."

I flop back in my chair with a stupid grin on my face. It's one thing for me to plan on a future with Samantha—it's another to have my family's support. It's a boost that shows me I'm making the right decision even though it's a hard one.

Dad stands up, scanning us. "Now..." He claps his hands, rubbing them together. "I'm hankering for a steak your mother probably won't approve of, and a few too many dark ales I *know* she would not approve of."

He heads to the door with Matt in tow.

Fin comes over and offers me his hand. "You alright?"

Clasping his hand, I let him tug me up. "Yeah, just surprised."

I collect my keys, phone, and wallet, then turn to him. "You could have given me a heads-up."

He slaps my back, harder than necessary. "Now, where would the fun be in that?"

"Asshat," I mutter.

He laughs. "Hey, you know if it was going to be bad news I would have had your back, right?"

"Yeah, I know. But you didn't have to enjoy my stewing so much."

"Ah, stop being such a pussy."

With that one glorious word, my mind goes back to Samantha. I've been called a pussy a lot in relation to my feelings about her. I don't even give a shit anymore. I take it as a compliment, because if she makes me softer, kinder when it comes to her, then I'm all good.

Now, I need to stop being such a whiny ass and take control of our situation. I need to be proactive in my approach instead of being reactive.

Dad said love. I wasn't sure if I was there yet, but now I have no doubt I am.

I love her.

Now, I need to be the man who deserves her.

Sixteen

Samantha

"HEY, DAD, WHAT'S UP?" I ANSWER MY PHONE, still in bed.

"My morning surgery was canceled, leaving me with a little extra time I'd love to spend having breakfast with my daughter. Meet me at our usual place?"

He probably called my mom first, but she had an important meeting this morning. I don't hold it against him. It's my dad, and everyone takes second fiddle to my mom—him, his job, and even us kids. "Sure." I hang up and rush around like a madwoman so I can meet him and not be late for class. Luckily, I have a free period this morning, so if I'm late it's not the end of the world.

It's just a perfectionist thing in me. I'm never late, at least not since I've been in control of my schedule. In elementary school I was late a few times due to my parents running behind. They quickly realized I didn't need their help to get ready and turned their efforts toward Jace and themselves, knowing I'd be in the car waiting for them. And I was, every day, until I was old enough to drive myself.

I manage to make it out the door in under fifteen minutes. I don't have any makeup on, but most days I only wear mascara and lip balm, and I can do that in the car on my way to school.

Ten minutes later I'm pulling into the diner parking lot. I find my dad's car right away, but there's no parking spots near him. I continue to the back of the lot, park, grab my purse, and rush inside.

I spot him in a back corner booth. "Hi, Dad." I give him a kiss on the cheek. His skin still holds his tan from Hawaii a few weeks ago.

"Hi, pumpkin." He gives me a quick squeeze before I sit across from him. "You made good time." He studies me for a moment, his smile softening into a tender look of love. "You're beautiful. You remind me so much of your mother when she was your age."

My mother is a beautiful, sophisticated woman. She is all the things I don't feel I am. "Dad, you didn't know mom at my age."

"Psshhh, I saw pictures. And I knew her a few months after she turned eighteen. You're nearly eighteen. Practically the same age."

He motions the waitress over so we can order. "Where has the time gone?" he asks wistfully. "It's hard to believe you're basically the same age she was when I fell in love with her."

"You mean when you *both* fell in love?" I tease.

His laugh warms my heart. "I fell before your mother. It was pretty much love at first sight for me. She needed a little more convincing." He takes a drink of coffee. "I had a reputation back then—she doubted my ability to commit to her."

I love hearing Dad talk about how they fell in love. His eyes light up and shimmer in a way they only do for her.

"And you? You didn't doubt it?" It sounds like he's talking about Joseph and me. Joseph is my father, and I'm my mom. The similarities are striking, except the whole lover boy reputation is not Joseph's reputation.

"I've never doubted it for a second, Sam. I'm telling you, the minute I laid eyes on her, I was done for. I only had eyes for her from there on out. I still feel the same way. There's no one else. There never will be."

The smile on his face says it all, how happy and content he is. It must be a wonderful feeling to be so certain and feel so loved.

"I love that about you, Daddy. The way you love Mom. The way you never shy away from telling her or anyone else." I avert my eyes. I don't want him to see them fill with tears.

"'*Daddy*.' You haven't called me that in a long time. I've missed it." He smiles. "What's to be shy of? It's not weak to love a woman. In fact, it takes tremendous strength to love and commit to another person for life. I want that for you, Sam. Based on what I saw over Thanksgiving and the avoidance I've seen since, I think you've found it. A little earlier than your mother and I did, but not by much. I sense you're afraid, but you don't need to be. I see the man Joseph is, the man he will be. I see the way he looks at you, the way he treats you. He'll make you a good husband."

"Daddy! We're not even seeing each other," I admonish.

Stop! Just Stop. I don't need you feeding my hopes and dreams. I do it enough on my own.

"Don't let fear stand in your way, pumpkin. You'll be eighteen in a few weeks. Old enough to make your own choices, not that you're not mature enough now, but people tend to listen more when your age equals your maturity. But you've always been more mature than, well, all of us, I think. Don't let your mature ways scare you off from what's right in front of you. Have a little childish hope and belief left in you to see the life you could have with him."

I'm thankful when our food arrives. I brush my tears away and focus on eating and enjoying these precious moments with my dad. The rest of our conversation is more lighthearted as he tells me about an interesting case of a child he operated on yesterday. I get lost in his passion for his job and his patients. If you'd never heard him talk about my mom, you'd think *this* was his first love, but it's a close second. Though, he'd say it's Mom, me and Jace, and then his job. In that order—no arguments.

When we finish it's nearly 8 AM. I've got thirty minutes to make it to class. I excuse myself to brush my teeth and freshen up in the restroom before heading to school.

Dad's waiting for me by the door when I come out. He gives me a big hug. "I'm glad you made it, Sam. It's good to have this time to catch up."

"Thanks for inviting me." I decide not to mention I know he probably invited Mom first. There's no point in making him admit it. Plus, there is nothing wrong with him inviting Mom before he did me. It's the way it should be.

Someday I hope to be someone's first choice.

As we exit, he heads toward his car, and I point to the back of the parking lot. "I'm over here. I'll see you when I get home from work tonight."

"Alright, have a good day. Kick ass, Sam."

I just laugh and shake my head. "You too, Dad."

"Hey, what happened to 'Daddy?'"

"I grew up." I keep walking to my car.

"You're never too old to call me Daddy, pumpkin," he hollers across the lot.

"Goodbye, Daddy," I yell back, ending this ridiculous conversation. I chuckle to myself as I approach my car. As the humor wanes, my mind wanders back to what he said about Joseph. I'm surprised by his observations and that he's telling me to go for it instead of telling me to focus on my education. I guess he wants me to have what he and Mom have.

My key fob in hand, I unlock the car.

"Sam."

My motion falters as a familiar bone-chilling prickle raises the hairs on my neck and sends shivers down my spine. His German-but-not-exactly-German accent is too distinctive for it to be anyone else. The same dreaded voice from months ago.

Before I can turn around, something hard presses into my back. This time I don't hesitate. I hit the panic button on my remote, setting off my car alarm.

"Stupid bitch," he hisses in my ear, too close to be drowned out by my car alarm.

He spins me around. I'm not surprised to see the man who used to sit at the bar at my work and approached me months ago in the parking lot.

He backs away from my car, motioning me to do the same. He's holding a gun pointed at my chest. "You never told your father. Why not, Sam?"

He's right. I never did. My dad was out of town when it happened, and by the time he was back, my panic had subsided. I decided to wait and see if I saw him again. When he never showed, I assumed it was just some bizarre prank.

"Sam!" My father's voice booms from behind me. I don't take my eyes off of the man with the gun.

"Ah, Daniel, so nice of you to join us." He points the gun at my father.

"No! Please, don't shoot him," I plead.

The man laughs. "I don't intend on killing him, Sam." He redirects his aim at me. "Now you, on the other hand, are a different story. Daniel…" He glances over my shoulder. "Step closer so I can see you, but not too close."

We're in the back parking lot, secluded between two buildings. It's not very likely anyone will come upon us unless their car is parked here.

My dad comes into view to my right.

"It's okay, Sam," he says softly.

No, it isn't. My palms are sweaty, and my pulse pounds in my ears. I'm determined to remain strong and not be a distraction or a hindrance to my father dealing with this man.

"Roderick, let her go. She has nothing to do with this." Dad's voice is full of conviction.

Roderick laughs again. "Daniel, Daniel, Daniel, you should have listened to me. It's too late for bargaining. You should have given me what I asked for. Now you have to choose between protecting your patient or your daughter."

Dad moves closer to Roderick, putting himself between us. "She's just a kid. Let her go. I'll give you what you want, but you need to let her get in her car and drive away. I'm not helping you as long as she's in danger."

I don't think I've ever heard my dad's voice be so commanding. If I were this man, I'd do as he says.

Roderick shakes his head. "You're still trying to manipulate me, Daniel. There are no negotiations here. You will go to your office and get me what I want. Then I will release your daughter."

Dad steps closer. "No," he says firmly.

Roderick's face turns hard, impassive. He cocks the gun still pointed at me. "No? I will shoot her, Daniel. I have killed those more important to me than her. Don't push me."

Dad steps closer. "Roderick, I will help you. I said I would. You don't need to threaten my daughter's life." His eyes flick to me quickly. "Sam, get in your car."

"Daddy," I whimper, my gaze teetering between him and Roderick.

"Do as I say, Sam." His voice brooks no argument, but I can't make my feet move. I'm pinned in place by fear.

"Move and I will shoot you and then your father," Roderick barks.

The threat is evident, yet instead of feeding my fear, it bolsters my confidence. I step forward, grabbing my dad's hand. "You won't have time to shoot both of us. If you shoot me, my dad will be on you so fast you won't know what hit you. If you shoot him first, then I'll be on you just as fast. I may not be as strong, but you won't take me easily."

My dad squeezes my hand tightly in a show of solidarity. But all I want to do is wrap myself around him and disappear.

Roderick's face twitches into a twisted smile. "You have balls, girl. You should be proud, Daniel. I've watched her for many months. She's a good girl, strong, independent, but maybe not so smart."

"I am proud." Dad slowly pulls me behind him. "I couldn't be more proud of her. Please, Roderick. Let her go."

"Hey! What the fuck?" A deep voice comes from the side of the building.

I chance a glance as a burly man comes into full view rounding the corner.

Roderick pivots quickly, his gun follows, pointing at the man.

I want to yell at the guy to *look out*, but before I do, my dad yells, "Get down!"

The gun jerks in Roderick's hand a split second before the shot rings out, echoing as if in slow motion, hitting the side of building, barely missing the man's head as he ducks behind a parked car.

"Sam." Dad's face encompasses my vision as he abruptly turns, diving to cover my body with his.

His face and my name on his lips are last thing I remember before the gun goes off again.

PART 7
THY WILL BE DONE

Seventeen

Joseph

A RINGING PHONE JERKS ME AWAKE, MY HEART pounding as if it was a siren blaring in the room. I arrived home from class and laid down to rest my eyes for just a few minutes. An hour ago. I guess I was more tired than I thought.

I stretch as I reach for my phone on the nightstand. "Hey, Dad." I stifle a yawn. I don't want to sound like a total slacker.

"Joseph." His use of my full name has my attention immediately. He only uses it when I'm in trouble or he's about to be terribly serious.

I also hear the strain in his voice. "What's wrong?"

"I just got off the phone with Eleanor," he says solemnly.

I sit straight up in bed, my gut filling with dread. "Mrs. Cavanagh?" I clarify. Maybe he means a different Eleanor—not Jace and Samantha's mom.

"Joseph—"

"Fuck, stop calling me that. You're gonna give me a heart attack. Did something happen to Samantha?" It can't be Jace. I just talked to him before I laid down.

"I don't have all the details..."

Fuck. Fuck. Fuck.

"...Sam was having breakfast with her father. Some man pulled a gun on them—"

"Christ, no!" I stand up and pace. "Please, Dad, tell me she's okay." Panic surges through my body.

"She's okay, son. Or she's going to be—"

"What the fuck does that mean?" I throw my bedroom door open and charge into Jace's room just to be sure he isn't here. He's not.

"Joseph, I know this is hard, but let me get this out before you jump to conclusions."

"Yes, okay. Sorry." I stop in the living room and sit on the edge of the couch.

"Both she and her father were shot."

Oh Christ. Jesus. No!

I squeeze my eyes shut, waiting, just waiting for him to finish.

"Sam's in surgery. They expect her to recover."

I let out a breath and open my eyes, seeing stars for a moment. "And her father?"

"He died, Joseph, I'm sorry to say." Dad's in tears.

It's my undoing. I start to cry even though I need to hold on tight and get to Dallas to my girl.

"Dad," is all I can manage.

"I know, son. It's a horrible situation. But Sam's going to be okay. That's something to be thankful for." His voice is comforting, and I wish I were already home.

"Does Jace know?" Dread fills me thinking of his reaction.

"Eleanor was calling him as soon as I hung up with her. She called me because...well, she wanted to get you boys home as quickly as possible. It's a tough situation. She needs to be strong for her kids, but she also just lost the love of her life. We're going to help get them through this," he says with absolute certainty. "Listen, the jet is on its way to you. You and Jace just need to get some clothes together for a week or so and get to the private airport. It'll be there waiting for you. It's faster and safer than you two driving home."

"Thanks, Dad. I appreciate it. Do Fin and Matt know?"

"They just walked in my office. I'll fill them in. I wanted to tell you first, get the ball rolling with getting you both home."

I'm in a daze, not sure how to proceed.

After a moment of silence, my dad's voice interrupts my thoughts. "Joseph, you need to get a move on. The faster you get your stuff together, the faster you'll get to see Sam."

"Yes, you're right."

"I love you, son. And I'm really sorry about this. We'll get through this together. All of us."

"I love you too."

After we hang up, I sit for a moment envisioning the conversation he's having with Matt and Fin. Then I think of Jace. I hope his mom is able to reach him. If I don't hear from him in fifteen minutes, I'm going to call him. I need to give her a chance to be the one to tell him. Sometimes we need that connection from a parent we just can't get from friends, no matter how close we are.

I'm in the middle of packing when my phone rings. "Jace. I'm so sorry, brother."

"Joe." His voice cracks, struggling to keep it together.

"I know, man. We'll get through this. Focus on getting home to pack. My dad sent the jet. It'll be waiting for us."

He lets out a sigh of relief.

"We'll take it one step at a time. You're not alone. I've got your back. *We've* got your back."

I finish packing and start getting some of Jace's stuff laid out on his bed. He's not going to be thinking straight, so I'm trying to think for him.

I've done all I can and start to pace in the living room. Watching the minutes tick by is pure torture.

I call Fin.

"We've got you. Matt and I are almost to the hospital. Victor will meet your plane." He rattles off the facts like a to-do list, which is surprisingly comforting.

"Samantha…" I choke, not able to tell him what I really want to say.

"Joe, man. We've got her," Fin says.

"Concentrate on getting home. Let us focus on what's happening here in Dallas," Matt chimes in.

"I'll text or call with any news," Fin reassures.

"Thanks."

"You're welcome, brother."

I hang up, still anxious. I need to get home to my girl.

My Sweetness.

Joseph

Jace and I were a mess on the flight home. He more so than I. I was only stressed over Samantha. Jace was dealing with the loss of his father, his sister getting shot, and a mother who's even more of a mess than he is. I tried to console him, be his rock. But I was lost in my own thoughts most of the way here.

A herd of cattle couldn't have kept me away from Samantha once we reached the hospital. Thankfully, no one tried to stop me. We were greeted by my dad and brothers as soon as we walked through the waiting room doors.

Dad takes Jace in his arms as soon as he's within reach. Jace buries his face in my dad's shoulder and starts to cry. My dad just holds him tighter. "It's alright, my boy, let it out."

I sigh in relief. Dad thinks of Jace as his fourth son, which is exactly what Jace needs right now.

I move to Fin and Matt, hugging both of them close, taking a moment to remember how important they are to me. I fill with a sense of peace and thankfulness for my family being here. They're a deep well of support, not just for me, but for Samantha, Jace, and Eleanor too.

Fin fills me in. Our moms are keeping vigil by Samantha's bedside—she's out of surgery, but hasn't regained consciousness. With the blood loss and sedation, they don't expect her to fully wake up for a while. They haven't seen her yet, but it's good news she's not in the ICU.

Deciding to give Jace the time he needs with my dad, I make my way down the hall to Samantha's room. I knock on the door but don't wait for a response before I open and close it quietly behind me. Mom is sitting next to Eleanor, holding her hand. They're just sitting, too deep in thought to hear me knock.

Mom sees me first and relief spreads across her worried face as she takes me in. "Joe," she sighs. "I'm so glad you made it." She meets me halfway across the room and wraps me in her arms.

"Nothing could keep me away." Though her head hits me mid-chest, she is the one hugging me, comforting me. I hold her tightly.

Eleanor stands, shakily, and makes her way to us.

I release my mom with a quick squeeze. "Mrs. Cavanagh, I'm so sorry," I choke out before enveloping her in my arms.

"Thank you." She pats me softly. "Sam will be so happy to see you. She woke up earlier and asked for you."

My heart soars—even in her sedated state she's thinking of me. "Does she remember what happened?"

Mom comes back to my side. "She wasn't awake long enough for us to determine what she remembers. She said your name and fell back asleep. The nurse said it could be hours before she wakes up for any length of time."

I release Eleanor and steel myself for my first good look at Samantha. She's lying in the hospital bed. Her head and knees are elevated, IVs in her left arm, oxygen tube in her nose, and machines at the head of the bed where all those tubes seem to connect. Her hair's spread out over the pillow as if she's peacefully asleep. Pale, but still beautiful.

Sitting on the side of the bed, I hold her left hand in mine. "How is she? I mean, where is she injured and what did the doctor say?" I need all the details so I know what we're dealing with.

Eleanor moves back to her chair and rests her hand on Samantha's leg, but only closes her eyes instead of answering my question. She's heartbroken, obviously.

My mom sits back down and gives me a reassuring smile. "She was shot in her right shoulder. Miraculously, the bullet only nicked her collarbone and passed straight through, missing any major arteries. There's tissue damage and she'll have scars, but both should improve over time."

Samantha's right arm is in a sling, her hand resting on her chest. I touch her hand lightly and trail my fingers up to the top of her hospital gown. I can just make out a bandage under the neckline. I pull it back enough to see more of the bandage covering her shoulder. I study it for just a moment before covering her back up, continuing to trace my fingers down her jaw, and then cupping her soft, warm cheek.

My Sweetness.

I close my eyes, trying to compose the mixture of emotions rising in me. I want to cry for her loss and anguish over the death of her father as well as her own trauma. I want to get on my knees and thank God for sparing her life. I want to crawl in bed with her and never let her go.

"Eleanor, why don't we go see Jace and leave Samantha in Joe's care? He'll let us know when she wakes up. You've had a long day and need to get some rest yourself. There's a chance she may not even wake up tonight. You should get some rest while you can," Mom suggests.

Eleanor only takes a moment to study Samantha and then me. "Yes, she's in good hands." She nods and gets up.

My mom meets my eyes. "I'll send Fin in to answer your questions."

"Thank you."

I promise to contact them the moment she wakes up or if I have any additional news.

Not even a minute later, Fin comes in the room followed by Jace. I study Jace for a quick moment as he settles into the chair his mom vacated. He's haggard, worn out.

Fin comes closer. "The doctor said the surgery went well. She lost a lot of blood, but she's young, in good health. They expect her to recover fully."

I have questions. I don't want to make this harder on Jace than it already is, but it can't wait. "What happened? Tell me everything."

Fin sits next to Jace. "An eye witness says he came upon them in the parking lot. A man was pointing the gun at Daniel, who had Samantha behind his back."

Protecting her. He was protecting her.

I look at my sweet girl and squeeze her hand. I can only imagine how scared she was.

"The witness yelled out and the guy turned and shot at him. He didn't get hit, but he dove behind a car and didn't see what happened next. He only heard the second gun shot. By the time the assailant ran off, the witness found Sam on the ground with her father in her arms. She was busy caring for her father, as were the EMTs when they arrived. No one checked her out. They all assumed the blood on her was from Daniel. It wasn't until she passed out they realized she'd been shot too."

Christ.

"Until the police obtain the video surveillance and Sam wakes up, we won't know any more details, unless another witness comes forward," Fin concludes.

Jace leans forward, his eyes locked on Samantha. "The witness said he heard a *second* shot, assuming one more. If he only heard one, how did both my dad and Sam get shot?"

I was worried he'd shut down on us. I'm happy to see him present and thinking.

"The working theory is that given your father was shot in the heart—his left side, and she was shot on her right, the police believe your dad turned to face Sam just as the other shot was fired. The bullet hit him first and then continued into Sam. With their height difference it's a reasonable conclusion."

"Do we know…" Jace chokes back a sob.

Fin puts an arm around him. "It's alright, man."

Jace shakes his head, as if he's trying to dispel his emotions. "Did my dad die immediately?"

Fin nods with a grimace. "The EMTs said he was already gone by the time they got there." His eyes lift to mine before continuing. "He was shot in the heart. It would have been pretty instantaneous." He seems to ponder for a moment before continuing. "He didn't suffer long, if that's what you're concerned with."

"That's something, I guess," Jace mutters.

My eyes focus back on sleeping beauty. "She saw her father die." My voice is low, almost a whisper in reverence for what those words hold.

"Yes," Fin's reply is nearly as soft as mine. "The police said the EMTs had to pry Daniel from her arms. She was holding him tight, rocking him against her chest."

"Jesus," Jace vocalizes my sentiments.

I smooth her hair from her forehead, caressing her face as gently as possible. "She's gonna be a mess."

Eighteen

Samantha

BLINK MY EYES IN THE DIMLY LIT ROOM. MY HEAD pounds like little coalminers are trying to dig their way out. My entire body hurts, even to breathe. It takes me a minute to clear the fog from my brain. I look around slowly, my head rioting against any quick movements.

Jace is lying in a bed a few feet away on his side facing me, sound asleep. Peaceful.

I scan my body, noting I'm lying in a bed similar to the one Jace is in, but there's a weight on my legs. My heart lurches at the sight of Joseph asleep with his head in my lap. My hand is resting on his cheek. Did he place my hand there or did I? Did I need his comfort, the contact, even in my unconscious state?

Joseph.

Jace.

Why are they here?

I survey the room, needing more clues.

Damn fuzzy brain. *Think!*

I've got nothing.

I hate to do it. I hate to wake him up. I flex my hand on his cheek. His stubble tickles my palm. If I weren't so groggy, I might have giggled.

"Joseph," I manage to croak as I run my fingers along his silky dark mane.

"Hmm?" he mumbles, opening his eyes, blinking up at me. "Sweetness." He immediately sits up. "You're awake." He seems relieved.

Shakily, I touch his face. I'm so weak. He places his hand on top of mine, holding it securely against his face.

"I'm so happy to see you." The pained emotions behind those words are apparent, but he doesn't really look happy.

Why?

"Why are you here?" I peer over at Jace and then back to him. "I don't…" My thoughts fumble for the reason I'm here.

Joseph captures my hand in his. "It's alright, baby. You've been asleep. Give yourself a minute to wake up. Adjust."

"Where?" I manage.

He nods. "You're in the hospital, Samantha. Do you know why? Do you remember what happened?"

His smooth voice is comforting and melodic. I close my eyes for a moment before opening them. "Talk…to me."

A small, sweet smile dons his lips. "You want me to talk to you?"

I nod, grimacing as my head revolts.

"Are you in pain?"

"Head. It's my head." I close my eyes, thankful for the dark.

I hear the beep of an intercom and Joseph speaking to someone on the other end.

Panicking, I open my eyes to confirm he's still here, to focus on him. I squeeze his hand. "Don't go."

My eyes slip closed despite my desire to keep them open.

Soft lips brush against mine. "I'm not going anywhere, Samantha. Rest. A nurse will be here in a minute to help with the pain."

I mumble my response, at least I think I do. I'm not sure.

I'm starting to drift.

A soft female voice and a gentle touch wake me up. I open my eyes to kind gray eyes watching me.

"Ms. Cavanagh, I'm Charlotte, your night nurse."

Nurse?

I nod, though I'm not sure why. It feels like I should acknowledge what she's saying even though I don't really comprehend what it means. Why would I need a nurse?

She asks me a list of questions about my physical state. I do my best to answer.

On my right, Joseph stands, watching me. "Joseph."

He smiles. "Yes, Sweetness."

"You're here."

He chuckles. "Not going anywhere. You can stop being so surprised each time you wake up to see me here." He moves closer, touching my cheek before his lips press to my nose. "I'm not leaving you. I promise."

Thank, god. "Good."

"Ms. Cavanagh." The nurse brings my attention back to her. She's holding up a cable with a button on the end. "This is for your pain meds. You can push it every fifteen minutes—more than that and nothing will happen. I would recommend you use it so you stay ahead of your pain. At least for the next twenty-four hours, I wouldn't wait until you're hurting to press it."

She holds up her hand. "I brought you a pill to help with your headache. Do you think you can swallow it?"

"Water," I croak.

She smiles and holds up a cup with a straw, bringing it to my mouth. I take a drink and then swallow the pill, finishing off the water.

She leaves with the promise to bring me back a tumbler with ice water along with some chicken broth.

Am I hungry?

Joseph gently massages my temples, running his thumbs across my brow, down my cheekbones, along my jaw and back to my temples. "Rest, baby."

He does it over and over again, slowly, tenderly, with just a hint of pressure.

I succumb to his healing touch as my eyes flutter closed.

"Samantha." Joseph's deep voice pulls me from sleep, his hand gently caressing my cheek.

I open my eyes to him sitting on the bed at my side. My eyes are still heavy, it's hard to keep them open.

"I'm sorry to wake you." He holds up a mug with a plastic lid. "The nurse brought some broth. I thought you might like to try to drink it while it's still hot."

"Kay," I manage with tremendous effort.

He punches a straw through the lid and takes a quick sip, making a satisfactory nod of approval. "Not bad."

Pressing the straw to my lips, he offers, "Small sips. It's hot, but not too hot."

I take a tentative pull on the straw, relishing the warmth as it coats my raw throat, which feels like I swallowed sandpaper.

Joseph continues to feed me, alternating between drinks of water and chicken broth until I've had enough.

I notice Jace is gone from the bed he was sleeping in before. *How long ago was that?*

"I sent him home." He smiles, grabbing hold of my left hand. "It's just you and me tonight." He bends down and kisses my forehead. "How's your head? Better?"

It takes me a second to remember why he's asking. I nod. "It's better." My voice is smoother but still crackling with the effort.

He frowns. "Your throat's sore, isn't it?"

"Dry. Scratchy."

"I'll get you some throat lozenges. It should help."

Pulling out his phone, he steps away and quietly asks someone to bring some lozenges, cough drops, or hard candy, anything to help my throat.

He hangs up, watching me watch him, and returns to my side. "Fin's going to bring you something for your throat."

I frown. "No. Don't trouble him."

"It's no trouble. He's here anyway. He brought me dinner and was just hanging out a while in case you needed anything." My confusion must show on my face. "I ate while you were sleeping."

Sleeping. The thought prompts a yawn I try to stifle.

He gives me a knowing look, bending down to kiss me. His lips are soft and tender against mine. Pulling back, he seems sad, his voice chock-full of emotion. "Rest."

He kisses me one more time, then moves to solemnly peer out the window into the night sky. His jaw clenches, and his hands are tightly fisted at his sides.

"Joseph," I call to him.

His eyes meet mine over his shoulder. "Rest, Sweetness. I'll still be here when you wake up. Promise."

"No."

His brow arches and then softens into a true smile as he stalks closer. "No, huh?"

"What's wrong?" I'm nearly in tears, and I don't know why.

His cups my face, his thumb caressing my skin.

"Shhh." He leans down capturing my mouth once again. "You can hardly keep your eyes open. Rest, Samantha. I promise to not leave you, but I need you to sleep now." He kisses my forehead, then sits on the side of the bed. "Close your eyes."

Reluctantly, I do as he asks. It won't take long for me to sink into slumber.

His warm, strong, capable hands begin to massage my face and head as he did before. But this time with no additional pressure, just light tender soothing touches that have my shoulders relaxing and thoughts drifting off...

Joseph

It didn't take long for her to relax under my hands and fall asleep. Fin arrived shortly after, having bought lozenges for her throat in the gift shop. He stayed for a while to visit, keeping me company, and helped me move the extra bed to the other side of hers. I want to be closer to her, but not block access to her injured shoulder, as the nurses will continue to come in and check on her through the night. In the end, I settled on her left side, my bed nudged right up to hers.

I intend it to stay there until someone tells me I need to move it.

I settle in, having brushed my teeth and changed into shorts and a t-shirt. I lie here watching her, her hand nestled in mine, her breathing soft and content. Her face is lax and has more color than it had when I first arrived. Her right arm is bound by the sling resting on her rising chest. She's a dream, an angel, and a heartbreak waiting to happen.

She's been too drugged to remember, to comprehend what's happened. She seemed to accept she's in the hospital and is apparently happy to have me by her side, which boosts my confidence tenfold for being the one to stay with her. Jace wanted to stay, or he felt like he needed to stay, but his mom needed support too.

I, on the other hand, *wanted* to stay almost more than I *needed* to.

My need is far different from Jace's, though. While we both love her in different ways, his need comes from obligation as her brother and now being the man of the family. My need comes from a much deeper and perhaps darker place. Mine comes from the need to protect what's *mine*.

Part of protecting her is to be here in any way she needs me to be, and if it's as her nursemaid, then give me scrubs and sign me up.

Mine to protect.

Mine to hold.

164

Mine to comfort.

Mine to heal.

Mine to love.

Mine.

I close my eyes as that word races through my mind, filling every empty thought, empty craving, empty promise, empty memory. Thoughts of her fill me to near capacity. I fear I will detonate from the sheer force of all those empty *everythings* being expelled from every cell of my being.

Mine.

Hers.

Hers to protect.

Hers to hold

Hers to comfort.

Hers to heal.

Hers to love.

Hers.

I. Am. Hers.

I'm roused from sleep by screaming, my hand gripped in a vise.

"No!" my girl screams.

Adrenaline rips through my body with as much power as her next scream. "Daddy, no!" She's still asleep.

"Samantha," I call to her, moving as quickly as I can, half-lying on my bed and hers, pulling my covers, still tightly wrapped around my legs, with me.

"Wake up," I plead with her thrashing, whimpering form.

With another jarring move she screams in pain as her injured shoulder takes the brunt of her escapades.

I move closer, wrapping her in my arms, avoiding her right arm and shoulder as much as possible.

"Samantha, wake up," I say firmly and sigh in relief when she starts to relax in my hold.

"Joseph." The pain in her voice guts me to my core.

She remembers.

My girl remembers.

"I'm here, Sweetness." My tears fall, mixing with hers as she sobs in my arms. "I'm here."

I'm here.

I'll always be here.

Nineteen

Samantha

THERE'S A SOLEMN MOOD COATING MY WAKING state. Tears are never far from my eyes. I feel up-ended and drained physically, mentally, and emotionally.

I remember.

I remember it all.

I should be sad. I should prefer not to remember, but I can't bring myself to feel that way. Those were the last moments of my dad's precious life, and it's a burden I will gladly carry. It should be *my love* carrying them and not the murderous heart of the man who took his life.

The police have come and gone. They accurately surmised most of what happened. I filled in the rest.

If they know who Roderick is—they aren't saying.

If they understand his motive, what information Dad had that the killer wanted—they aren't saying.

They aren't saying much, actually. They want me to give and give so they can take and take.

I stand for it. I allow it, as if I have a choice. It's the only hope we have for answers. For a reason for my father to be dead that makes sense—even though nothing could justify or truly explain it.

My hospital room is full of remorse and sadness from my mom and brother. Understandably so, but difficult to breathe through. They were here when I woke this morning, their obligation to be here heavy in the air. I feel the weight of it, and it's oppressive.

Joseph is hovering...hovering...hovering.

Agitation crawls up my skin. I can't stand it. I throw back the covers, swinging my legs over the side of my bed, grimacing and biting back pain from the sutured hole in my shoulder. The hole from the same bullet that killed my father.

Fuck. That hurts.

Joseph jumps up. "Christ, what are you doing?"

He's in front of me faster than I can move, stopping my progress. "I'm going for a walk," I bark, pushing his hands away.

"Wait. Just wait." His voice softens as he kneels low enough to see my downcast face.

"Sweetness." His tenderness is unhinging, and my traitorous tears begin to fall again.

I peer at him, roughly wiping at my face, sneaking a glance at my family, who watch me with bleary-eyed despair.

"I have to get out of here, or they need to leave—or both," I whisper.

He nods. "Let's take a walk, then maybe they'll let me take you outside in a wheelchair for some...fresh air."

I sigh with relief. He understands. I need to get away for perspective more than fresh air.

Joseph talks quietly with Jace and my mom, suggesting perhaps I've had enough of visitors for a while. I escape to the restroom. When I come out, they give me gentle hugs and quick goodbyes, seemingly relieved to be leaving.

Robe and slippers donned, Joseph and I make our way out of my room.

He takes my hand, twining our fingers with a need to be in constant contact with me since I woke up last night screaming, screaming as I relived the events that stole my father's life away.

"Do you think maybe next time you need a break you could tell me instead of hurting yourself to get out of bed?" He glances sideways at me, watching, calculating my reaction and his response.

I sigh. "Yes, I suppose I could." He seems satisfied by my answer, yet I'm not. "I can do this Joseph. You don't have to stay. I appreciate you being here and all you've done for me. But I can take care of myself."

I've been doing it my whole life, it feels like.

He squeezes my hand. He's calm like he expected me to say as much. "Just because you can take care of yourself doesn't mean you have to, or that you should." He repeats his sentiments from our first dinner together.

We stop at the end of the hall. Before heading back, he pivots in front of me, still holding my hand. His free hand snakes in my hair, tugging gently to lift my face to his. "Samantha, you're not alone. I'm here. I *want* to be here. Let me."

His eyes bore into mine trying to drive home his point. I think there's more he wants to say, but he remains silent. He left me in silence for so long…but he's here now.

I nod once.

Satisfied, he presses a kiss to my forehead before we resume our walk down the hall.

It's a long day with multiple walks and visits from Margot and Joseph's family.

Margot stays to help me with a shower. The nurse offered but was convinced to let Margot and Joseph handle it once I confirmed I was okay with it. Keeping my wound dry is a challenge but Joseph is good at applying the water proof covering the nurse provided.

My robe drapes open at the collar to reveal my wounded shoulder. Joseph tenderly kisses along my neck, pausing at my ear. "Are you sure you don't want me to help you shower, Sweetness?"

I muffle a moan and shudder at the thought of him having his hands all over my wet body. My elation is marred by the pain that shoots through my shoulder. I wince with a whimper.

He grips my waist, bracing me against him, sighing. "I'm sorry. I shouldn't have done that." Turbulent green eyes meet mine.

"I'm not. It was hot." I kiss his cheek, thankful that on this day, full of so much sadness, he finds a way to make me feel desired, cared for yet not pitied.

I join Margot in the bathroom where she's been setting up, getting everything ready.

She jokes, helps me relax and not feel self-conscious about sitting naked in a shower chair as she washes my hair, alternating handing me soap and rinsing me off as I wash my body.

She ends up getting pretty wet in the process. If she weren't so tiny, she could have worn some of my clothes my mom brought earlier. But as it is, she heads home for dry clothes and a date with Bobby, Sebastian's friend.

Sebastian came by today. He was on duty in the ER this morning when he heard news of a trauma that came in yesterday, on his day off, of a father/daughter shooting. Nobody besides me had his number, and honestly, calling people was not anywhere on my list of concerns. Out of curiosity he checked the computer for notes of the trauma as a learning tool. He was shocked to find out the daughter was me. He was livid when he showed up at my hospital door, but relaxed when he laid eyes on me and saw that I was okay.

I was worried how Joseph would respond to him, given his response in January when he thought I was on a date with Sebastian. Joseph couldn't have been any nicer. They actually talked about Sebastian joining the next Six-Pack poker night. I'm not sure if I should be happy about that or be upset he's no longer jealous of Sebastian.

I'm pouting when Joseph comes back from walking Sebastian out. *Is he my friend or Joseph's?*

Joseph stops in his tracks. "What's that look for?"

"You!" I point at him in frustration, standing up from the chair I've occupied for the last hour. "You nearly mauled me at the restaurant the last time you saw me with Sebastian, and now you're...you're like best buds. Do you want to date him?"

His toothy, dimpled smile only infuriates me more, which makes him throw his head back and laugh that rich, deep laugh of his.

Ass!

He cocks his head and stalks toward me, gently wrapping me in his arms. "Sweetness, are you upset I'm not acting all jealous? Is that what this is about?"

"Hmph," I reply, picking at invisible lint on his broad, muscled chest.

He leans down. I feel his smile, even though I can't see it. He kisses my jaw, and then tilts my chin so he can see my eyes. "Do you need me to ravage you against the wall like I did last time to make you feel better?"

My insides clench in hopeful anticipation.

Jesus, what's wrong with me? I've been shot, and my father just died. "No."

His all-too-knowing smile is back. "Sebastian and I came to an agreement. Therefore, I trust him to keep things as just friends. But make no mistake, Samantha, I will rip any man's head off if he tries to touch you."

"Oh." Fuck. That's sexy as hell.

His lips brush mine. "Yes. '*Oh*.' Are we good?"

I nod, still trying to get my bearings.

"Good." He notices my still-wet hair clipped on top of my head. "Why don't you let me dry your hair, and then we can curl up on the bed and watch a movie. How's that sound?"

I rest my forehead on his chest. His hands caress my back, and I let out a deep sigh. "It sounds like heaven."

PART 8
SAVING GOODBYE

Twenty

Joseph

I LEAVE HER ON THE COUCH WITH JACE AS I HEAD TO the kitchen to get us some food. Fin and Matt are sitting at the island eating, drinking beer. The guests have all left; only immediate family remains, hers and mine. The funeral and reception are finally over. I can breathe again. It's been a hellacious week. Samantha has been a trouper through it all, pulling more than her own weight. Jace and Eleanor have been in a daze. I'm sure if I wasn't here, if my family wasn't here to help out, they'd step up more. At least I hope they would. But, I'm not willing to take the chance and leave Samantha all on her own. Plus, there's nowhere else I'd rather be than by her side in whatever capacity she needs.

"Hey," I say to Fin and Matt, wondering how they'd react if it was our father who was killed. Would they shut down or would they step up and be the men I believe them to be?

"Hey," they reply in unison.

"How's Sam?" Matt asks.

"She's okay. She's hanging out with Dad and Jace at the moment. I need to get her some food."

Fin motions around the kitchen to the assortment of foil covered to-go containers, glass casserole dishes and the like scattered around. "Take your pick."

"The lasagna is really good. There's salad too, if you think she'd like that," Matt offers.

175

I put together a couple of plates for her and Jace on a tray with some drinks, napkins, and any other items I think they may want or need. After I take it to them and get her settled with promises she'll actually eat, I return to the kitchen to visit with my brothers.

I grab a beer and some food, then join them at the island bar. I take a couple of bites and have to agree with Matt, the lasagna's really good. Sometimes, there's nothing like good old comfort food to hit the spot.

"Thanks guys for being here today, this week. We couldn't have gotten through all of this without you both." In all sincerity, that's the truth. Beyond keeping the place packed with food, running errands, helping with funeral planning, Fin even worked with Samantha's principal, after approval from Eleanor, to get her school work sent home and organized a tutor if she needs help.

They try to brush me off, downplaying their parts.

After a few minutes of companionable silence, Fin speaks up. "She's a great girl, Joe," he says pointedly.

I meet his eyes. "Yes, she is."

"She's crazy about you," he says.

My beer stops midway to my mouth. "I'm just as crazy about her."

"She's a tender soul. Be careful there." His eyes are fierce with protectiveness for her and that gets my back up.

"Fin, is there something you want to say to me?"

"I just did," he says dryly.

"Why are you getting all bent out of shape?" I finish off my beer and get up to dump my paper plate in the trash. "You know how I feel about her. We've talked about this, probably more than we should."

He lets out a breath, running his hands over his face. It's been a hard day for all of us. "Look, I don't mean to be a dick, really. I'm just worried about her. There's a sorrow, an emptiness. I'm worried you being all *Mr. Practical*, and *it's not our time*, will break her."

Until You **SET ME FREE**

"I can't fuck this up." My shoulders sag at the thought.

They both mutter their agreement.

I lean against the counter. "She needs my support now. That's why I'm here." I stare at the wall as if I can see her on the other side. "That, and the fact there's no way I wouldn't be here for her or Jace. I don't want to hurt her, but I don't want to lead her on either. I can't give her the future she deserves yet."

"Joe, I don't disagree with anything you've said. I'm just saying, her father dying makes it more complicated, makes her more apt to get hurt. Be sure, no matter what you do, she knows *why* you're doing it. It might make it an easier pill to swallow."

"Maybe you need to rethink the whole timing thing," Matt chimes in. "Isn't she gonna be eighteen soon, anyway?"

"Yeah, in a few weeks. But it's more than that, she needs to focus on college and what she wants to do with her life. I don't want to be the reason she doesn't pursue her dreams, her aspirations. I want to help her become who she's supposed to be, not be the reason she doesn't become it. She needs time to experience life." I wish I had the answers, an easy fix.

"Wherever she ends up, isn't that where she's supposed to be?" Jace's voice sounds from the doorway, his brow arched in question.

"Okay, Buddha," I tease. I take the tray from him and hand him a beer, figuring he could use it.

"Thanks," he says, making his way to the island to sit by Matt. "She went in to see Mom, in case you're wondering." He smirks at me, knowing that was in fact the next question out of my mouth.

Dad comes in shortly, and we discuss the plan for the next few days.

The weight of this day and the conversation we just had hangs heavily on my mind.

Samantha

I slip into my parents' room. Mom's asleep, which I figured she would be. I need to see her, if only for a few minutes. I close the curtains and move to close the ones on the French doors that open to the backyard. Instead, I find myself standing there, admiring their semi-private garden. I sit on the chaise lounge in front of the doors, lost in thought. My father had this private area put in a few years ago, to give them privacy when their curtains were open and not feel like anyone in the pool could see directly into their room. I thought it was a really romantic gesture. Something I imagine having someday, maybe even with Joseph.

Mom stirs, and I turn to see her watching me.

"Mom?" I move closer. "I'm sorry, I didn't mean to wake you."

She frowns. "No, your father woke me." She touches her lips. "He kissed me and told me to wake up." Her sad eyes roam his side of the bed. "That obviously didn't really happen."

Oh, god. I swallow the lump in my throat and sit on the edge of the bed, holding her hand. "Can I get you anything? Fresh water? Food?"

Her eyes slip back to mine, trying to focus through the haze of her sleeping pills.

"Sam." She cups my cheek. "Your father was always so proud of you. He'll be really angry when he realizes he's going to miss seeing you grow into the woman you're destined to be, finding your way, making a life and a family of your own."

"Mom," I plead as tears begin to fall again. They seem endless these days.

She squeezes my hand. "In some way, he'll see you. I'm just sorry it won't be in the tangible way he had always planned. He was looking forward to walking you down the aisle when you marry Joe."

"That's not...you don't know if that will happen. He...just don't talk about Joseph like that. It's too painful to think about, especially if it never happens."

Patting my hand, she leans close. "Sam, life is too short. Don't let that man get away from you if he's the one you choose." Her gaze turns to the French doors. "I know what I'm talking about. I never thought I'd be a widow in my forties."

Overcome with emotions and unwilling to break down in front of her, I hurry to her bathroom, blow my nose, and splash water on my face. When I open the door, Jace is sitting on the edge of the bed where I just vacated. He brought her some food.

I put my hand on his shoulder. He snakes his arm around my waist, pulling me onto his lap. "How are you holding up?"

I nod and try like crazy not to cry. My chin starts to tremble, and I'm going to fail miserably. I quietly cry on his shoulder as he rubs my back. "It's okay, Sam. You don't have to be brave. It's okay to cry."

That makes me cry even harder, and then I hear my mom's heart-breaking sobs. *No.*

I jump off Jace's lap, moving the tray of food out of the way. He moves closer and pulls her into his arms, and then wraps his arm around me, holding us both, as I hold both of them.

It's a heartbreaking thing, to hear your parent cry with such sorrow, such loss, such hopelessness. I don't blame her; I don't think I could stand to lose Joseph, and we are nowhere in the same place that my parents were. They were each other's soulmates, their other halves. She's faced with having to live the rest of her life missing half of herself. It's frightening for me to even consider my future without my dad in my life. I can't even fathom the depth of despair she's feeling. I can empathize, but I can't truly understand the magnitude of it.

To top it off, there's my brother, who's the happy-go-lucky-life-of-the-party guy, but tonight he's breaking. My older, stronger, tougher-than-me brother is crying. I don't blame him. I don't think less of him. There is no shame in his tears. It is just hard to witness. It puts the reality of the situation front and center.

I don't know how we move on from here. I don't know how we know-ingly, actively move forward without my father. He wouldn't want us to stagnate, stay where we are in loss and grief, but the knowing and the reality of the action is daunting, to say the least.

I slowly pull away, kissing them both on the head, and take Mom's tray of food to the kitchen. She's not going to eat it, at least not now.

The house is quiet. Joseph's family must have left. According to the clock in the kitchen, it's only nine, but it feels so much later. I'm exhausted. I take one look at the kitchen and know I'm not going to bed anytime soon.

I turn on the water, open the dishwasher, and start to rinse and load the dirty dishes. I'm lost in thought, or maybe I'm lost in no thoughts at all, when I feel strong arms around my waist.

"Sweetness." Even he sounds sad.

He's been my rock this week, in the hospital and out. I've tried continually to distance myself from him, but he continually pushes through my barriers, knocking them down one by one.

"Don't be nice to me, Joseph, or I'll start to cry again. I don't think I can take anymore today," I warn.

He kisses my neck and squeezes me gently. "Tell me what I can do to help."

I glance over my shoulder at him and around the kitchen. "We have to find a place for all this food. Can you throw away what's nearly gone or not worth saving? Maybe make a place for things that don't need to be refrigerated. Then, when I finish the dishes, I'll start making room in the refrigerator."

"I'll make room in the fridge."

We work well together, organizing, tossing, combining food, making order out of apparent chaos. With my injured shoulder, it takes me longer than it would otherwise. I try not to think about it, ignoring the pain and weariness of my bones and aching muscles.

Of course, Jace comes in just as we finish. I start to laugh as soon as I see him.

"What?" he says, his blue eyes red-rimmed and completely confused by what I find so humorous.

With the back of my hand over my mouth, I try to stop, but I just can't. "I'm sorry, it just struck me as funny that just as we finish cleaning up such a mess, you come strolling in."

He stands there, arms crossed over his chest, annoyed. "I was actually coming to get something to eat. I'm still hungry."

I start to laugh harder.

He looks at Joseph, who only shrugs. "Hey, if you make a mess, you better clean it up."

More laughter.

Joseph captures my hand. "You're getting punchy, Sweetness." He pulls me into his side, wrapping his arm around my back with his hand resting on my hip. "How's your mom?" he asks Jace.

"She's resting now." Jace's sad smile says it all. He surveys me. "You okay, Sam? That was a little rough in there. I heard a little of what she said to you before you went into the bathroom."

"Yeah." My laughter silenced.

His eyes shift to Joseph and then back to me. "Do you want to talk about it?"

I shake my head. "No, Jace. I really don't."

"Okay," he says.

I grab his hand. "I love you." And slip out of Joseph's embrace to give Jace a hug.

He hugs me back, his head sinking into my hair. "I love you too, sis."

We stay like that for a few moments, then I ask him. "What do you want to eat? I'll get it for you."

He pulls away, a true smile on his face now. "Really?"

I chuckle. "Yes, really. Besides, we just cleaned up, and you're a bit of a tornado in the kitchen."

Joseph laughs behind me. "God, don't I know it."

Surprisingly, with all the food we have, Jace wanted bacon and eggs. I wasn't going to deny him, after all he buried his father today too. Joseph ends up wanting some. I make enough for the four of us, in case Mom wakes up and wants something later. I get the boys fed, wrap a plate up for Mom, make mine into a sandwich and leave the two of them visiting while I go shower.

Twenty-One

Samantha

SLIP INTO BED AS JOSEPH ENTERS THE ROOM ONLY wearing workout shorts. I lie on my side, pulling the covers up under my chin.

The bed dips behind me, and his warm body envelops me from behind.

I ask him the same question I ask every night, hoping I'll get a different answer. "Are you staying?"

"No." He nuzzles my neck, as his hand moves to my stomach, pulling me flush against him.

I'm turned on and disappointed at the same time.

"I can't stay in your room, Samantha. It wouldn't be right. I want to." He kisses my neck and chuckles when I shiver. "But, I can't."

I lay my hand over his. "My mom won't know. She's out of it right now."

He props up and tenderly pulls me to my back. His eyes lock on mine as he runs the tips of his fingers down the side of my face. "I'd know. And you'd know. I care too much to treat you that way." His lips graze my shoulder. "Now, roll back over and let me hold you for a while. I'll stay until you fall asleep."

I settle back on my side, wrapped in his arms, my back pressed to his front. How he can do this and not get turned on?

Slowly, my eyes get heavy, but a persistent thought keeps nagging me. "Joseph," I whisper, unsure if he's asleep.

"Sweetness." His sexy voice is so sure, so close, so comforting.

"If you're going to break my heart, please do it sooner rather than later." I clench my jaw, trying to keep my emotions from overflowing for the umpteenth time today.

He squeezes me tighter. "I'm not going to break your heart." He kisses along my injured shoulder.

"I just don't think I'd survive losing you too." My voice cracks and tears start to fall.

"Please don't think like that." He pulls me so tight, I think he'd crawl under my skin if he could. "I won't ever lie to you, baby. But I also won't promise you the moon when I'm not in the position to give it to you, not yet."

I sniff and wipe away my tears. "I think I can live with that."

He chuckles. "Good, 'cause I don't think I'd survive losing you either."

"I can definitely live with that."

"Good," he says softly.

"Good," I agree.

"Now, go to sleep. You know I need my beauty sleep."

"Goodnight, Joseph."

"Goodnight, my beautiful blue-eyed Sweetness."

Joseph

Jace catches me in the hall as I'm slipping out of her room. I run my hand nervously through my hair, knowing how it appears. He follows me into the guest room.

"So you're sleeping with her?" He's riding the edge of anger.

I close the door, so we don't wake up Samantha. I lean against it, facing him, trying to stay calm. It's been a really shitty week for him.

"No, Jace. I'm not sleeping with her." I cross my arms over my chest. "I wouldn't do that to her." Pushing off the door, I move closer to the bed. "We're not even messing around, except maybe a kiss here or there." I slump against the headboard. "She's hurting, just like you are. I want to be here for her, comfort her, be strong for her, be whatever the hell she needs me to be. But I'm not going to take advantage of her or the situation." Waving my hand. "Hence, why I'm in here instead of with her."

He sits on the end of the bed. "You'd rather be sleeping with her than staying in here?"

I almost laugh. *Is he serious?* "Is that a trick question?"

"No, I'm trying to judge where you're at. What she is to you." He runs his hands over his face and falls back on the bed. "I overheard my mom talking to her tonight. I only caught the tail end of the conversation before Sam disappeared in the bathroom, crying." His eyes fall to me. "My mom's hurting." He motions in the air. "Obviously. Who wouldn't be? She just lost the love of her life, the man she married when she was just nineteen and still in college. Just a year older than Sam and a year younger than me.

"Anyway, she was telling Sam how much our dad is going to miss watching her grow up, become who she's meant to be, and walking her down the aisle when she gets married..." His focus on me intensifies. "... to you."

"Shit. Your mom actually said that?" No wonder Samantha was upset tonight, talking about if I'm gonna break her heart, do it now and not later.

"Yeah, she did. Look, my parents love you, they love your family. They weren't blind. They saw what was happening between the two of you at Thanksgiving. And in the hospital, you stepping up to take care of her. I see it too. I think anyone who's around y'all for a few seconds can see it." He sighs and sits up, resting his arms on his knees. "The problem is, Sam doesn't believe it."

Shit.

That's ridiculous. I've told her she's mine; she knows I'm hers and that I just need more time. She knows how I feel; she has to. "What do you mean, she doesn't believe it?" My voice is eerily calm, not reflecting my inner turmoil in the least.

"I think she's *afraid* to believe may be more accurate. She told mom to stop talking about it. She couldn't stand to have those thoughts in her head, especially if they don't come true."

"She has a point, Jace." I get off the bed and start to pace, needing to move.

"Okay, now what do *you* mean?" His eyes bore into me.

"I mean…Fuck…Jace, she's a virgin, barely even been kissed. She's crazy smart, beautiful, compassionate…I could go on and on. But she's still young, not even eighteen. She's never had a boyfriend, barely any life experiences. You expect me to make a lifelong commitment to her now, before she's barely even started to live her life? Before she's who she's meant to be? It's like claiming her life before she has a chance to live it."

Awe, Christ, I'm gonna hyperventilate. I bend over, gripping my knees.

He presses his hand to my back. "Calm down, man. We're just talking here. I'm not accusing you, honest. I'm your friend, but I'm also her brother and her best friend." He laughs. "I see it now. It's destined to be, my two best friends, getting together, making a life for themselves."

"I wish it were that simple," I say, straightening up.

Studying me for a few uncomfortable moments, I notice for the first time he has the same blue eyes as Samantha and in some way, it is like I'm staring back at her.

"Joe, you're truly the nicest guy I know. You're incredibly smart too, but sometimes, you're a dumbshit. Maybe, it *is* as simple as that. Maybe what Sam is destined to be is your wife, and you her husband. Life, love, relationships, is not about what job you have. What Sam does, or will do for a living, is not who she is. And maybe, just maybe, she's not destined to be a tramp like me, but a one-man woman with you." He heads for the door. "Think about it." He opens the door and then pauses, not turning around. "Planning is all well and good, until it's not. Your life is happening right now. You're cheating yourself out of time—and no one knows how much we get. Don't miss out on what's right in front of you while you're planning for your future."

"She's not even eighteen, Jace," I whisper to his back.

"She will be in a few weeks. You and I both know she's more mature than most adults." He turns, pinning me with his stare. "If you don't want her, then don't be with her. Make it a clean break, and do it now. But if the only reason you're not taking the bull by the horns is because of her age, her inexperience, then that's crap."

I stifle a chuckle. "Are you telling me to sleep with your sister?"

He doesn't take the bait. "No, I'm tell you to grow a pair and don't fucking break her heart."

Joseph

A warm body brushes against me, stirring me from sleep. I open my eyes, blinking, trying to focus. "Samantha?"

"I didn't mean to wake you," she rasps, moving a little closer, but not quite close enough.

I reach out and pull her flush against me. "If you're gonna be in my bed, at least come cuddle with me properly."

She lets out a low giggle. "There's a proper way to cuddle?"

"There is when it comes to you and me," I say with all seriousness.

"Oh yeah, and how's that?" Her voice is light with humor.

I wrap her in my arms, pulling her close to my side with her head on my chest. "As close as humanly possible." I tilt her chin up to gauge what's really going on. "What's wrong, Sweetness?"

It isn't until the words are out of my mouth I realize what a stupid question it is. *Her father's dead, and she's been shot. For fuck's sake…that's what's wrong.*

She lays her head back on my bare chest, her hand resting over my heart. "I just woke up and couldn't get back to sleep. My mind started racing, thinking about all that's happened. I...I just didn't want to be alone."

Of course, she didn't. I run my hand up and down her bare arm. "Do you want to talk about it?"

"Not really. Can I just be like this with you for a little while?" she asks softly.

"For you, my arms are always open for business." I kiss the top of her head.

"Business? Is that what I am?"

"Far from it," I scoff.

After a pause, she lets out a long breath. "Then what am I, Joseph?" Her voice is low, seductive even. It does things to me.

I run my hand down her back, and she arches into me, pressing her breasts against my side, letting out a small whimper.

Christ, she's going to make me hard in two seconds flat.

"You're my future, Samantha."

"What if I can't be the person you want?" she whispers, finally giving voice to her fears, letting me in.

Ridiculous. "What do you mean? You're already the person I want."

"You're the Ivy League boardroom CEO, man of the world, and well, I'm not."

"So?"

She shakes her head. "Can you picture me on your arm at company parties, fundraisers, schmoozing with the business, political, and social elite? Being the perfect wife who always knows the right thing to say?"

"No." I laugh. She tenses in my arms, but I hold fast. "You think I want that? Sweetness, I love your mind. Our compatibility. We're going to rule an empire together. Don't you dare relegate yourself to trophy wife material. That's not who I want."

"Oh." The tension leaves her body all at once as she finally understands my plans for us. I run my hand up and then down her back again.

Each time I hit her lower back, she presses against me, then sighs, not in exasperation, but in pleasure.

"Please, stop doing that." Her voice, barely a whisper across my chest, makes my nipples hard and my cock stir.

I smile and do it again.

This time she wraps her arm around my waist and holds on as she squirms. *Christ.*

"Please," she says softly.

"Why? Why do you want me to stop?"

"Because."

"Because, why?" I run my hand down her back, stopping in that magical trigger spot, and trace circles across her heated flesh.

She presses against me, burying her head in my chest. "Joseph," she moans my name.

Christ almighty, my cock just got hard as steel hearing her say my name like that.

"Do you want me to stop because it turns you on?" My desire is evident in my voice.

"Yes." Her lips brush my nipple, and my cock twitches for attention.

"Does that embarrass you?"

"Yes." Her voice is barely audible.

"Do you have any idea how much it turns me on to know you're turned on?" Before she can answer, I gently roll us, taking her injured shoulder into account. I settle on top of her, my erection pressed against her.

"Is that your…" She can't even finish that statement. I have no doubt she'd be bright red if there were enough light for me to see.

"Yes, Sweetness, and it's all for you." I run my lips just barely across hers. "You're so beautiful, Samantha. You made me hard the second you walked in the kitchen that Friday before Thanksgiving break. All confidence and sass, and yet incredibly innocent and vulnerable at the same time." I press my lips to hers for a tender kiss.

As I pull away, she flicks her tongue out and licks my lips. I growl and go back for more, this time taking her tongue captive. She's going to be the death of me, I just know it.

Our lips lock together in an endless dance of need, want, and desire.

"Samantha." I break our kiss, moving to flick on the nightstand lamp, and pause to take in her heavenly face. The desire in her eyes nearly bowls me over.

"Am I hurting you?" I motion to her shoulder where her bandage is visible under her barely-there camisole.

"No. It's fine. Just don't ask me to put my hand over my head," she teases, trying to make light of her injury.

I kiss her shoulder tenderly. "I don't want to hurt you."

Her warm hand brushes my cheek. Our eyes meet and hold. "Joseph, the only part of me you're likely to hurt is my heart."

So brave. Always so brave. Facing her fears head on. *My girl.*

"Not gonna happen, Sweetness. I'm never letting you go."

I kiss her before she can verbalize what the shocked expression on her face means. I know she doubts me, my intentions to be with her for the long-term. I'll just have to prove it to her.

She moans as I deepen our kiss, holding her close.

My girl. I could have lost her.

I groan at the thought, my body at war with itself, wanting to just hold her and make her feel safe, reassure myself she is safe. And wanting to bury myself deep inside her, claiming her, making her mine.

My girl.

I stutter kisses across her face. "Do…you…want…to…stop?"

Her hands stop my kisses. I rise up to meet her gaze.

"No, don't stop." She lifts her lips to mine and plants a soft supple kiss, pulling away, sucking on my bottom lip, and then releasing it with a *pop.* "Don't ever stop."

Christ. I just got harder, if that's even possible.

I don't bother hiding my growl as I take possession of her mouth.

She moans in response, and it makes me want to please her more, turn her on more, do whatever is necessarily to hear more of those sexy as hell sounds of hers.

Her hands leave a blazing trail on my back and arms, pulling at me, urging, inciting my desire. I lay kisses down her neck. She arches, giving me free access to suck and lick my way to her ear.

"Wrap your legs around me."

My cock pulses from the sounds coming from her mouth and the feel of her glorious body beneath me.

She's only wearing panties and a camisole, and I'm in my boxer briefs. As much as I want to rip her clothes off, I'm not willing to take her virginity on the night she buried her father, nor am I willing to take it on a whim, even when most of my blood is taking up residence in my cock.

She slowly wraps her legs around my calves, rubbing her feet up and down my legs, pulling at me.

I adjust, settling my cock against the wet spot on her panties. "Look at me."

Her eyes meet mine.

I watch her face as I move my hips against her. She feels so good below me, better than I dared to imagine, and the need on her face tells me all I need to know.

"Joseph," she beckons in that sexy voice of hers.

"Let me take you there, beautiful." I grind harder, deeper, groaning when she moves her hips against my cock in rhythm with me.

"That's right, Sweetness. Show me what you need."

"Oh, God." She sounds desperate.

I ravaged her against the wall after New Years, but it was not nearly as intimate as this.

My girl.

"I got you, baby." I capture her lips, letting our bodies express how we feel for each other.

This is the beginning of something big, something important for our lives. I took to heart what Jace said earlier. I can plan the hell out of my life, her life, but if we're miserable for the next several years, is it worth it? When we can be together sooner, make a life together in the near future, isn't that a good thing? I'm not going to ask her to marry me tomorrow, but I'm done fighting what I've been fighting for months.

Her body starts to tremble, tensing with her imminent release. Her head falls back, breaking our kiss.

"Christ, you're sexy." I tweak her nipples as I grind against her. She circles her hips, bringing me along with her.

"Let it go, Sweetness. That orgasm you're holding onto is mine. Let me have it." I growl in her ear, barely managing to hold out for her.

She lets out a guttural cry, and I quickly stifle the sound with my mouth, swallowing her pleasure as she comes, quaking below me, continuing to move her hips with me, kissing me as if I'm her lifeline to her next breath. Her hands squeeze my ass, pulling me tighter against her.

The tingle starts in my balls, moving up my spine. I grind every bit of pleasure out of her orgasm as I fall into my own explosive release. "Samantha, fuck." I groan as my cum pumps across our bellies.

I don't stop grinding, and before I recover from my orgasm, she spirals into a second one, seemingly just as powerful as the first. I suck and pull on her nipples, prolonging her release as long as I can, relishing hearing my name on her lips as she comes for me.

I kiss across her face, chest, and neck as she recovers, not quite ready to break away from her to clean us up.

"You look entirely too proud of yourself," she taunts.

I chuckle. "I was just wondering if I'm the first to give you an orgasm. Obviously, not this time, but the time before." I'm almost embarrassed, thinking that I may have given her her first orgasm and in a public place nonetheless.

She rolls her eyes. "You have a thing for my firsts, don't you?"

I capture her face in my palms. "You have no idea."

"Would it make you happy if I say *yes?*"

I remember her saying those exact words when I asked if I was the first to touch her lush breasts. I give her the same smile I gave her then, one of complete satisfied accomplishment.

"Are you going to slowly claim each part of my body? Each of my firsts?" she asks.

"Oh, Sweetness, I have every intention of making every inch of you mine." I repress the desire to growl and bite her neck in total possession. I want every single one of her firsts.

My girl.

PART 9
DREAMS AND NIGHTMARES

MARCH

Twenty-Two

Samantha

JOSEPH AND I ARE OFFICIALLY SOMETHING. IT'S yet unnamed. Though he has introduced himself as my boyfriend instead of just a friend, or Jace's roommate, or Jace's friend. There are a lot of titles he could have chosen, so I guess it's something that he chose the boyfriend title. He's just never said those words to me.

He's only been gone a few weeks, but it feels like a lifetime ago he was here taking care of me in the hospital and the week of my father's funeral.

It sucks that we finally make it official—but have to be long distance. I know he wishes he were here too, and that makes it a little easier. And we talk every day, so there's no more radio silence, and that makes a huge difference. I don't know how I'd have survived the last few weeks without him.

Relying on someone like this scares me.

It feels too perfect to be real.

There's a knock at the front door, and my stomach plummets. I dread opening it. To be faced with the reality of what's out there. Who's out there.

FBI Special Agent Michael Hennessey greets me with a stiff smile. I think he might be even more uncomfortable than I am.

I step back, letting him enter. "Agent Hennessey, come in."

"Please call me Michael, Sam." His voice is gruff and curt.

"Michael it is, then." I lead him into the kitchen, offering him a drink, which he declines. I get myself a glass of iced tea and pour a glass for him, ignoring his harrumph when I hand it to him.

Surprisingly, he ends up downing half of it in one large gulp, making me laugh as I quietly refill it.

"Thank you." I'm gifted with a genuine smile. He should do that more often. He's actually really good looking when he smiles.

"You're welcome, Michael." I want to give him a hard time, but decide to let it pass. If, however, he keeps up this hard-as-nails exterior, I may have to work extra hard to break through his icy façade for no other reason than to have some sort of connection with the man who's best friends with Fin and Victor, and has come to talk to me about my father's death.

"Sam, I realize this might be awkward, given we met previously on a more personal level, but today I'm actually here on official FBI business."

He says it was personal before, but I don't believe that to be true. He came with Fin and Victor to the hospital to visit me. I got the impression he was there as a favor, to unofficially check in on me and get his impressions of the situation with my father.

"I figured as much from your phone call yesterday."

"Director Sinclair would like to speak to you in the coming days, but I asked to speak to you first as a courtesy to Joseph and your ties to his family."

That rubs me the wrong way. I understand what he's saying, but it irks me all the same that I don't qualify for special treatment on my own—I only get it because of my relationship with Joseph.

If he notices my silent disapproval, he's doesn't acknowledge it. "As I mentioned on the phone, the FBI will be taking over your father's case. We'll continue to utilize some of the local PD resources, keeping them in the loop, but I'll be your primary point person going forward."

I cross my arms, still irritated by all of this. "And why is that?"

"Why will I be your contact?" He scoffs as if I've offended him. "I told you, because of your ties to the McIntyres."

I lean toward him over the table, hardening my voice. "No. I mean why is the FBI interested in my father's murder?"

He nods, not bristling over my tone. "Because of your father's involvement with the FBI at the time of his death."

All the air in my lungs whooshes out in a huff. I clench my fists in an effort to focus on breathing. It takes me a moment before I can speak. "What?"

This time he leans forward, his voice softer when he speaks. "This information is confidential, Sam. It's important it not be repeated. If anyone else is to know, I need to be the one to vet them."

"What about Jace and my mom?"

"I'll bring them in."

"What about Joseph and his family? They're the whole reason you're even here." I sound bitter.

"I deserve that I suppose, but, for now, no."

"No?" I repeat.

"No. They don't fall in the need-to-know column," he says simply.

"But they're the reason you're here," I protest.

"The irony doesn't escape me."

"I don't want to lie to Joseph." I cross my arms. "He'll know if I'm hiding something."

"I imagine this will be difficult for you to keep from Joseph, but it's in the best interest of his safety, and in the best interest of the investigation. The fewer people who know, the better."

Safety? "Is Joseph in danger?" My heart races at the idea of any of my loved ones being in danger, especially Joseph, who's become my rock. I already lost Dad. I can't lose anyone else. "What do you mean his safety?" I shoot to my feet as if I'm going somewhere.

His hand grasps my arm. "Stay with me. I won't let anything happen to Joseph or anyone else." He pauses until I focus on him. "I'm more concerned about you at the moment. You're the one the killer was stalking. *You're* the one he shot. We're putting you under protection, but you should be unaware of their presence for the most part. For now, I want you to continue your normal activities—work and school."

"Why me? And why was Dad working with the FBI? He's a surgeon, not a secret agent!"

Michael sighs. "The less you know, the better."

With men posted outside to *protect* me, he leaves, giving me his card and cell number, telling me to call him day or night with issues or concerns. And of course, if I spot the killer, to call him immediately.

Someone shot at me once. What if he attacked again while Joseph was here visiting, or even tried to get to me through him? If he got hurt because of me, I'd never be able to live with myself.

My throat burns.

I stalk to my room and grab my phone.

"Sweetness." Joseph's soothing voice fills me with regret as soon as I hear it.

"We need to talk." I start to pace the floor, trying to psych myself up for what I'm about to do.

"Shit. What's wrong?" See, even he knows those four words never mean any good.

I take a deep breath and brace my hand against the wall, leaning forward, my head bent, my eyes closed. This is for his own protection. "I can't do this anymore, Joseph. This long-distance thing is too hard. I'm not saying never. I'm just saying not now."

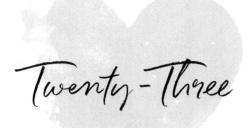

Twenty-Three

Joseph

"**F**UCK. FUCK. FUCK. FUCK. FUCK!" I BELLOW INTO the empty house.

Thankfully I had the foresight to not throw my phone, as was my first inclination when she ended the call. I speed dial Fin.

"Hey, Bro. What's up?"

"She fucking broke up with me." I pace into the living room, not fucking believing this. It's been a rough few weeks, but I considered it growing pains. Us feeling our way, trying to make the long-distance relationship work. But, I never thought she would break up with me, not like this, not over the phone and when we weren't even fighting. Other than the distance, we've been perfect.

"Tell me."

"There's not much to tell. She just called and said she can't do this anymore. She said the '*long-distance thing*' is too hard." I punch the wall. "Fuck! I can't believe this." I swallow the pain in my hand. Thankfully, I didn't hit the wall hard enough to put a hole in the drywall. The pain gives me a temporary reprieve from the pain in my chest and the sickness in my gut.

I drop to the couch, my head falling into my hand.

"What did you say?" His shock is apparent.

"I didn't say much. I tried to get her to talk to me, but she said she couldn't and hung up. It was obvious she was upset. I tried calling her back, but she didn't answer—it went straight to voicemail—she must have turned off her phone."

I stand and gaze blindly out the window. "Something must have happened. I don't know what, but I'm going to find out. My first guess is something to do with her father. Jace is at work, so I doubt it has anything to do with him. The police won't give me any details about the case. Can you talk to Victor or Michael? I'd call them, but I think they're more likely to tell you."

"Agreed. I'll speak to them and call you back. Victor is off for the night, so it might not be until tomorrow."

"Understood." I let out a sigh of relief. "Thanks, brother."

"Of course. Try not to worry. I'll call you back as soon as I have any news."

I head to the bar where Jace works to see if he has any idea why Samantha would break up with me for no apparent reason.

He sets a shot in front of me, as lost as I am as to why Samantha would break up with me out of the blue. "She didn't say anything to me. I'll call her when I get off work. See if I can find anything out."

I groan in thanks and toss back the shot. I relish the burn as it slides down my throat and warms my gut.

Jace sets another shot in front of me, motioning over my shoulder. "Tiff's over there. I'm sure she'd like to take your mind off your troubles."

"Are you fucking serious?" I swallow the next shot before he can answer.

Jace's has been a fucking mess since his dad's death. All the progress he made after Thanksgiving regarding dating women instead of just getting laid left and right has all gone to hell. He's back to his old ways. Actually, he's back to his old ways times two. I walked in on an orgy last week. He and three women right in the middle of our living room. Last night, he and our friend Davis disappeared with some girl into his room, doing god knows what. I assume they were double teaming her. I've never known Davis or Jace to swing both ways, but he's not himself right now. He's heartbroken and taking it out on his body, his sex life, and anyone daring enough to get near his dick.

He sets another shot in front of me. "Sometimes you gotta do what you gotta do to get by." He shrugs and moves to the other end of the bar, filling drink orders as he goes.

I down the shot knowing I shouldn't, but welcome the numbness that dulls the pain of losing Samantha.

"Come on, Joe. You gotta help me out a little here. You're like dead weight, and you're bigger than me as it is." Jace pulls me along with my arm wrapped over his shoulder and his around my waist. I try to focus on his face and his words, but both are difficult at the moment.

I stumble over the doorjamb to our house, catching myself before I slam into the entryway wall. "You're a good friend, Jace." My tongue feels too thick for my mouth, and my words are a slurred mess. I lost count of how many shots I had after the first seven.

"Yeah, yeah. Be a good friend and make it to your bed before you pass out, huh?"

"You got it, brotha."

He laughs as he dumps me on my bed. My eyes stay open long enough to see him yank off my shoes.

Joseph

"Ah sweets, that feels so good." Her tongue runs up the thick length of my cock, before circling the head with her talented tongue.

Fuck! Where'd she learn to do that?

Christ, I don't want to know that.

"Samantha, baby. Fuck." I groan as she swallows my cock, going deeper each time.

"Oh fuck. Yes." Her hot mouth consumes me over and over again. My hands fist the sheets to keep from sinking into her hair and pounding into her mouth until I come down her throat so fucking hard.

I moan at the thought, overcome by the vision in my head.

Then she's riding me, taking me deep. Her head is thrown back, lost in her own pleasure.

"That's right, baby. Make it feel good." I grip her hips as I thrust up into her, relishing her cries of ecstasy as she comes undone...for me.

She's gripping me, her hungry pussy sucking at my cock. "I'm coming, baby."

My head falls back, letting go, giving her all I have. Everything I have is hers. "Samantha."

Joseph

I wake up, my head pounding and my cock begging for attention. I roll to a sitting position, slinging my legs over the side of the bed, burying my head in my hands.

Fuck. I have to lay off the alcohol.

I stumble to the bathroom and turn on the shower, slathering toothpaste on my toothbrush and brushing vigorously while the water heats up.

As I shower the vision of my dream comes back to me, reviving my hard-on.

Christ, that dream seemed so real. What I wouldn't give for it to have been.

"Fuck."

I soap up my cock and fist it, reliving my dream. Samantha's sweet mouth and cunt all over me, eating me up. I rub one out, needing to savor the memory of my dream as the heartache of her words slams into me anew. *I can't do this anymore, Joseph…I'm not saying never. I'm just saying not now.*

"Samantha." It's a plea; it's an exultation as I come thinking of my girl in my fantasy and in my waking world where she doesn't want to be my girl. *I'm not saying never. I'm just saying not now.*

"Fuck," I grunt out as remorse fills my head and settles in my bones.

I quickly dry off, throwing on some athletic shorts, and stalk toward the kitchen in desperate need of coffee and aspirin.

"Hey, man," Jace greets me all too loudly.

I wince.

"That bad, huh?" He's amused.

Fucker.

"Worse. What was I thinking?" I swallow two aspirin and a full glass of water before tackling the Keurig.

He comes to stand next to me as I wait for my mug to fill with black gold. "So…I see you didn't turn Tiff away last night."

I huff out my exasperation, too hungover to deal with his happy ass this morning. "What the fuck are you talking about?"

He motions to my chest. "She's likes to leave her mark."

I study him for the first time today, really getting a look at his face. He's amused, but also guilty. "Jace, I know I'm hungover, but what the ever-loving-hell are you talking about?"

"Have you looked in the mirror?"

No, actually I hadn't. I kept the bathroom light off and my eyes closed most of the time. But I still don't know what he's talking about.

I stalk to the mirror in the entryway, seeing myself for the first time since yesterday.

"What. The. Fuck?"

I run my hands through my hair, pulling just enough to inflict pain. I need to be sure I'm awake. Realizing I am, I run my hand over my chest, over what I can only describe as claw marks: red vertical lines, down my chest, ending halfway down my abdomen. The skin is irritated with red puffy lines.

"Tiff likes to leave her mark," Jace says again, leaning against the wall, eyeing me. Now he looks guilty as hell.

"Christ, fuck." I sink to the floor as the realization hits me. "It wasn't a dream."

It wasn't Samantha.

It was Tiff.

And.

It.

Was.

Real.

"No. No. No. No. This cannot be happening." My head falls to my hands. "Jace, fuck, man. Please tell me that didn't happen last night."

My eyes burn with tears as I stare up at him.

He shrugs. "It's not cheating if she broke up with you."

"Are you fucking kidding me?" I bark.

"No." He backs up to the living room, scoping his options, like he needs to escape whatever's going around in his head.

Realization dawns again. "You knew."

I get to my feet and storm toward him. "Tell me you did not fucking send Tiff to my room, knowing I was completely shitfaced."

"You needed it, man." He backs up.

I press forward, pushing him just hard enough to make him fall back on the couch. "No! What I fucking needed was your sister. Not some random fuck from one of your leftovers." I loom over him, wanting to punch the hell out of his smug face.

Thinking better of it, I back up, running my hands through my hair. "Jesus Christ, Jace. What the fuck is wrong with you? Can't you see how fucked up this is? I was drunk out of my mind over your sister, so you send some girl into my room to suck me off?"

He points to my chest. "She did more than suck your dick. By the looks of it she rode you hard, holding on with her fingernails."

"Goddammit!" I can't fucking believe this. I collapse onto the adjacent couch, the grief and guilt hitting me full force. I close my eyes, letting my head fall back. "I didn't even know it was happening." I'm so fucked. How am I ever going to explain this to Samantha? Who would believe it wasn't my choice?

"You really didn't know?" His voice is almost unrecognizable and barely breaches my thoughts.

I don't look at him. I can't bear the sight of him. "I thought it was a dream. It was Samantha. The most amazing dream ever...a fantasy."

"Shit," is all he says.

"Imagine someone doing that to Samantha—sending some guy into her room when she's had so much to drink she's barely conscious. And he fucks her while she's lying there, thinking it's all a dream."

He swallows hard. "That's rape, man."

"Exactly. I didn't fucking consent to fuck Tiff. That's on her, but you're the one who sent her in there knowing the state I was in." I get up off the couch and stomp to my bathroom. I hold my breath before I look in the trashcan. Shit. I let out my breath. Thank god there's a condom and the wrapper sitting on top.

I can't believe this. I walk back to Jace, who's still slumped down on the couch. I'm determined to make this right. "Jace, I love you like a brother. But you broke something between us. I don't know if we can make this right, but I'm damn sure going to try to get Samantha back. If you can't get on board with that, then you need to stay the fuck out of my way."

I start to walk away.

"Joe."

I hear the regret in his voice. I stop, but don't turn around. "Don't. I can't deal with you now, Jace. You need to figure out your shit. You're falling off the deep end, and you have good reasons, but you have a mom and a sister who need you healthy and strong, not a lost manwhore, trying to corrupt his friends. Self-destruct by yourself. Leave me and your family out of it."

Heading to my room, I throw on a t-shirt to hide the evidence of last night.

I thought it was Samantha. I never for one second thought it was real, but the most amazing fantasy ever—that not only had she not broken up with me—but that she had given herself to me fully, completely, and without abandon.

Christ, fuck. This is a nightmare.

I can't tell Samantha Jace sent another woman in to… She's lost her dad. If she knew what Jace had done, she'd throw him from her life as well. She needs him—well, he needs to get his shit together first. But I refuse to take anything from her life. Which means I'll have to lie.

All I want is to make things right between us, but that means lying to her to salvage her relationship with her brother—if he doesn't self-destruct first.

I sit on the edge of my bed, taking a deep breath, and make the hardest phone call of my life.

Twenty-Four

Samantha

I HARDLY SLEPT LAST NIGHT. AFTER CALLING JOSEPH and breaking things off with him, I called in sick to work and did the same today. I can't even get out of bed. I made my choice, but it doesn't feel like a choice, it feels more like something done to me. I couldn't put Joseph in danger. There was no choice in that. I can't have what happened to my father happen to him. I'm thankful for the first time that he and Jace are four hours away. It's not far, but it seems safer than if they lived here.

Now I need to do the same with Margo, Sebastian, and my mom. I need to distance myself from them so they aren't in danger. I guess that includes Jace too, though he's been absent since Dad died. I doubt he'll even notice.

I couldn't live with myself if anything happened to any of them.

My cell ringing startles me out of my stupor. I don't even lift my head to see who's calling—I don't care to see who it is. I let it go to voice mail. A few moments later, it rings again, and then again. I finally reach for it to see who's so persistent.

Seeing as it's Michael, I decide to answer. "Hello."

"Sam, why aren't you at work?" His gruff tone is less than welcoming.

"I called in sick."

"Why?" He sounds angry.

"Why what?" I'm feeling obstinate. He brings it out of me for some reason.

"Sam, don't play games with me. Why did you call in sick? You aren't sick." His irritation is apparent.

"You know what, Michael, I have a parent, and though I just lost my dad, I don't need another one. I'm home. I'm safe. I'm not going anywhere. I'm also ending this conversation." I hang up, and it feels damn good.

It's not like me to be so mean, but I'm raw. I'm worn out, and I can't take his judgmental shit right now.

I roll over and fight the tears that keep coming.

My phone rings again. This time I answer it on the first ring without even looking. "What?" I nearly holler into the phone.

"Samantha?"

"Shit, Joseph. I'm sorry. I thought it was…" I don't want to tell him I thought he was Michael—it'll raise all kinds of questions I can't answer. I can't have him figuring out why I broke up with him. I harden my voice. "It doesn't matter. Why are you calling?"

"I have to talk to you, Sweetness." He sounds upset. I guess he should be if he feels half as bad as I do since we spoke yesterday.

"I can't right now." I start to hang up.

"Please. Don't hang up. If you don't talk to me now, I'll just come there in person. One way or another you're going to listen." He's obviously not going to be as easily deterred as Michael was.

"Okay."

He lets out a deep sigh. "I have to tell you something."

After a few moments of silence, I can't take it. "What?" I brace myself for him to plead with me to take him back. *Stay strong. He's safer far away from you.*

A strange noise comes over the line, a noise of anguish. I panic at the thought of him crying on the line with me.

"I slept with someone." His voice is so deep and pained. "I didn't mean to. I didn't set out to cheat on you. I got drunk…and, she…well… it happened."

My stomach twists and lurches. *Don't be sick. Don't be sick. Don't be sick,* I chant to myself over and over again.

"Samantha?" His voice breaks through my mental chant.

"When?" I manage before the tears start to fall.

"Last night."

Oh fuck! I rush to the bathroom, dropping my phone, barely making it to the toilet before I lose the contents of my stomach, which isn't much since I haven't eaten. That doesn't stop my body from continuing to try.

When the heaving finally stops, the sobs start. Having barely recovered from throwing up, my breathing is choppy and strained. I fall back on my haunches, my eyes squeezed tightly shut, causing stars to appear.

I can hear Joseph's voice in the background. I'd nearly forgotten he was still on the phone. I pull myself up, rinse my mouth and splash cool water on my face. I grab the hand towel to dry off and sink to the floor.

In the quiet stillness of the bathroom, I can hear the panicked echo of Joseph's voice. "Christ, Samantha, please pick up the phone."

More expletives escape before I reach for it.

I clear my throat. "I'm here." My raw throat protests my painful rasp.

"Ah, fuck, I'm so sorry. Are you okay? I mean, from getting sick, are you okay?"

I've never heard such worry and helplessness in his voice. It nearly breaks my heart as much as the idea of him having sex with another woman does. How could he move on so quickly? Did I mean nothing to him? And why is he telling me? Is this revenge for breaking up with him, and he's trying to hurt me?

"I'm sorry, Samantha. I can't tell you how sorry I am." He continues to say it over and over again.

"Joseph—"

"Please, please forgive me.

"Joseph—"

"I'm so sorry, Samantha."

"Joseph—"

"I didn't mean to. I didn't want to. I would never—"

"Joe," I nearly scream.

He stops talking, his less formal name getting his attention. Finally.

"Don't call me that." His pain is palpable.

He fucked another girl the day I broke up with him, and he's telling me not to call him Joe? "We weren't together. There's nothing to be sorry for." The chill in my voice is unexpected, even to my ears.

"Samantha," he pleads.

I drag myself to my feet, turning toward the haggard woman in the mirror.

Please, Daddy, give me strength, I pray as streams of tears roll down my face and onto my shirt.

Squaring my shoulders and shaking the tears away, I give one last attempt to set him free. "I can't do this anymore, Joe. I'm saying never." I hang up the phone, turn it off, and set it on the counter.

"Goodbye, Joseph," I whisper to no one, as there is no one to hear me.

No one to take away my pain, my sorrow, my loneliness.

It is just me now.

That's all I need.

That's all I've ever needed.

All I've ever really known.

I should never have believed otherwise.

I knew better.

Shame on me.

I climb in bed, nearly numb to the events of the last twenty-four hours.

Nearly.

But not nearly enough.

I'll give myself tonight to feel the weight of what I've just lost.

Tomorrow. Tomorrow, I will lock it all away and begin again without my dad, without Joseph, without Jace or my mom, without everyone I have ever loved.

PART 10
HAZE

Twenty-Five

Samantha

MICHAEL WASN'T AS EASILY DETERRED AS I thought he was. He scared the crap out of me when I woke up sometime Saturday evening and found him sitting in a chair next to my bed, reading on my tablet.

"Jesus, Michael, you scared me!" I gasp, shooting up, trying to catch my breath.

He chuckles, obviously finding my distress amusing.

Asshole!

"Serves you right for hanging up on me earlier," he says pointedly.

"Really?" I sit against the headboard. "You were being an ass." I throw a pillow at him. He catches the pillow without even looking. "How did you get in here anyway?"

"I'm a trained operative. I can do lots of scary shit, the least of which is breaking into a locked house with piss-poor security." His head tilts. "About being an ass, yes, I guess I was. I'll try to curb my assholeness in the future."

He sets the tablet on my nightstand and leans forward. "I was worried about you. You didn't show up for work on Friday or today. I guess I could have been gentler in my delivery, but you could have given me a heads-up. I had people in place ready to cover you while you worked. I was angry and I let it get the better of me. I'm sorry."

Wow. I did not expect a hard-ass like him to apologize so easily.

"Apology accepted. I'm sorry for not telling you. Honestly, it never even crossed my mind."

"You're forgiven. I should have been clearer on the context of our communication. So, we'll start fresh." He sits back in the chair, lifting his jean-clad legs and feet to rest on my bed. "What's wrong, Sam? Why didn't you go to work, and why are you still in bed?"

The concern in his voice brings tears to my eyes. I close them for a moment to temper my response. "How do you know I'm *still in bed?* I could have just laid down for a nap."

He shakes his head. "I came in to see you when I first got here, but decided not to wake you. That was six hours ago. Try again."

I throw back the covers and get up. I'm only wearing a t-shirt and panties, but I refuse to feel uncomfortable in my own bedroom. If he plans to come into my room while I'm sleeping, he's going to see me in what I sleep in. I am, however, thankful I'm wearing an oversized t-shirt instead of my normal cami. I turn to face him with only the bed between us. "I'd really rather not talk about it, if it's all the same to you."

He studies me for a moment and nods, having come to some conclusion I'm quite sure he's not going to share with me. "Fine." He stands up and moves to the door, stopping to glance back at me. "Put some clothes on and come downstairs. I've got dinner on the stove."

I peer down at myself, holding the hem of my t-shirt out like a skirt. "What? You don't like my t-shirt?"

His eyes scan down the length of my body before returning to my face. "Oh, I like it just fine, but I don't think Joe would appreciate me seeing you in such a state of undress."

I cross my arms over my chest, trying to alleviate the ache the mere mention of his name inflames. "Joe doesn't have any say in who sees me in any state."

His progress stops again, and he turns to face me fully. "What did you do?" His words are quick and intimidating.

"Why do you assume I did something?" I huff in response, trying to intimidate him right back.

"Because that boy is so in love with you, there is no way he wouldn't be pissed at me standing here in your bedroom," he says with certainty.

So in love he'd punish me by sleeping with someone else. You know, 'cause he cares so much. "I wouldn't bet on that."

He studies me for a moment before he moves, stalking, backing me up to the wall. "I'll ask again. What. Did. You. Do?" He eyes me with laser beam intensity.

I raise my chin and square my shoulders, refusing to be intimidated by him. "I did what needed to be done. And he did the rest..."

"Hmph," he says as he backs away, turning to the door. "We'll see," he mutters before closing my door behind him.

Joseph

My phone wakes me up early Sunday morning. My drunken hangover's gone, but has been replaced by my emotional hangover. I'm spent, wiped out, haggard as hell inside and out.

Fin's voice comes over the line before I even say hello. "The FBI has taken over her father's case."

He's got my full attention now. I sit up, shaking off my sleep fog. "When?"

"Michael went to see her Friday, late afternoon."

"She broke up with me on Friday."

"Yep."

"You don't think that's a coincidence, do you?" I'm beginning to see it's not either.

"Nope."

"Do you know why the FBI is involved?" My mind races, hoping I can turn this whole thing around. A part of me died yesterday when

I heard her getting sick over the news of me cheating on her—or her thinking I cheated on her.

Actually, I think a part of me died even before then when I realized it myself. I spent the day pissed as hell at Jace. It wasn't the truth, but I couldn't think of a better lie. I've still been plotting out how I'm going to make this right. How I can redeem myself for hurting her.

"Neither Victor or Michael are saying. Michael knows. He's the lead on the case. As for Victor, I'm not sure, but he's being tight-lipped either way."

"If the FBI is involved, it either means the killer is known to them or her father was," I surmise.

"I'm venturing it's both."

"What aren't you saying, Fin?"

He lets out a sigh, a rare sign of Fin's effort to keep his cool. "I don't know anything for sure, but a few months back when I mentioned you stayed with the Cavanaghs for Thanksgiving, Michael and Victor exchanged a look. At the time, I didn't really think much about it. Those two are always all cloak and dagger, it's par for the course with them. Then, Michael showed up at the hospital after the shooting. I assumed Victor had called him, to be there for us in case we needed him, but now, I'm not so sure."

Swinging my legs over the side of the bed, I hop up in one quick motion, reality having dawned. "She's protecting me. Michael thinks she's still in danger, which means anyone near her is in danger too." I pull on the nearest pair of jeans, placing the phone on speaker, then toss it on the bed. "She wouldn't want anyone to get hurt. She'll do whatever's necessary to make sure that doesn't happen, including breaking her own heart."

Fuck. My girl sacrificed everything for me, and I got hammered and…and everything got fucked up, but Samantha doesn't know that, and I'm not sure how to fix it.

"I would agree with that assessment."

"I'm calling Michael. In the meantime, can you put Victor on

Samantha? I want her covered 24/7. He can hire guys as needed. I know he's got the contacts. I'll cover the cost. Can you live without him?" Victor is Fin's right-hand man and best friend, but I trust him to do this right. I have no doubt Michael has her covered, but they operate in the realm of the government regulations; we don't.

"I'll manage. Consider it done." I hear movement on the line. "I'm glad to see you taking the bull by the horns, brother. I was worried after our last phone call," he admits.

"To be honest, Fin, things got a whole lot worse after we spoke."

"Worse than her breaking up with you?"

"Yep." I fill him in on my drunken night and the revelations of yesterday.

"Christ, Joe. You were…Jesus. Are you okay? Do I need to kill Jace?"

"I'm…dealing. Jace is punishing himself plenty, believe me." He's been so apologetic it's getting on my nerves. Words won't make what he did better—I'm going to have to get tested because of that asshole on top of everything else. At least his orgies have stopped…for now.

"And she must be devastated."

"I'm going to make it right. I'm done sitting on the sidelines and letting life lead me by the nose-hairs. This is my party, and I'm playing the next record."

He laughs. "That is a shit-ass analogy, but I get the point. You've been trying to logic your way into and out of this relationship since you met her. I'm glad to see you taking control. What else can I do to help?"

I fill him in on a few other ideas I have, but I'm not ready to move on those. He's on board though, which is a relief. As always, he has my back.

After we hang up, I finish getting dressed and head to the kitchen for coffee. The house is silent; either Jace is still asleep, or he didn't come home last night. I'm betting it's the latter. I'm still pissed at him, so it's probably best he's not here.

I call up Michael's number. He answers before I even hear it ring.

"Michael, you're on my shit list."

He chuckles. "It's about time you woke your ass up. Open your door."

I open the front door to Michael standing there with two coffee cups and a couple sacks of groceries.

"What are you doing here, man?" I take the coffees out of his already full arms.

"Putting my job on the line," he says as he passes.

I shut the door and follow him to the kitchen, knowing he's getting ready to lay some heavy shit on me. But I'm ready.

I'm ready for anything.

I'm ready to fight for my girl and our future.

The End

...well, not really!

Samantha and Joseph's journey continues in *Until You Are Mine* Book 2 in the *Until You* Series.

This is a dream for me to be able to share my love of writing with you. If you liked my book, please consider leaving a review on the retailer's site where you purchased this book (or on GoodReads).

Personal recommendations to your friends and loved ones is a great compliment too. Please share, follow, join my newsletter at mckdavis. com/subscribe, and help spread the word—let everyone know how much you loved Joseph and Samantha.

Acknowledgments

Thank you to my husband for your unwavering support and quiet cheer-leading while you text everyone that your wife is a published author. It's embarrassing but it also makes my heart flutter that you're proud of my accomplishments. To my children who make me feel like I'm conquering the world with each word I write.

You are my heart—I do this for you.

Special thanks to Teddy who never gives up on me and loves me through my silence. To Tamara for hand holding me through the editing process and for not dropping me when I'm quite sure she regrets taking me on. To the *Publish or Bust Gals* (Teddy, Shelly, Gayla) and the *M&M* Ladies (Teddy, TZ, Peyton, Pinkie) who saw *Until You* in the roughest forms and supported me anyway.

And lastly, to the readers—thank you for allowing me to share Joseph and Samantha with you. They've touch me deeply and drove me to write *what only the heart hears*. I hope you will tune in for their continued story in *Until You Are Mine* (dmckdavis.com/all-books/series/until-you/until-you-are-mine).

About the Author

D.M. Davis is a Contemporary and New Adult Romance Author.

She is a Texas native, wife, and mother. Her background is Project Management, technical writing, and application development. D.M. has been a lifelong reader and wrote poetry in her early life, but has found her true passion in writing about love and the intricate relationships between men and women.

She writes of broken hearts and second chances, of dreamers looking for more than they have and daring to reach for it.

D.M. believes it is never too late to make a change in your own life, to become the person you always wanted to be, but were afraid you were not worth the effort.

You are worth it. Take a chance on you. You never know what's possible if you don't try. Believe in yourself as you believe in others, and see what life has to offer.

Please visit her website, dmckdavis.com, for more details, and keep in touch by signing up for her newsletter, and joining her on Facebook, Twitter, and Instagram.

Additional Books by
D.M. DAVIS

Until You Series

Book 1—Until You Set Me Free

Book 2—Until You Are Mine

Book 3—Until You Say I Do

Book 4—Until You Believe

Finding Grace Series

Book 1—The Road to Redemption

Book 2—The Price of Atonement

Black Ops MMA Series

Book 1—No Mercy

Book 2—Rowdy

Book 3—Captain

Standalones

Warm Me Softly

Join My Reader Group

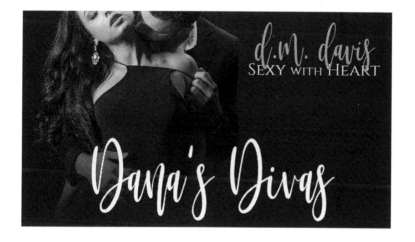

www.facebook.com/groups/dmdavisreadergroup

Stalk Me

Visit www.dmckdavis.com for more details about my books.

Keep in touch by signing up for my Newsletter.

Connect on social media:
Facebook: www.facebook.com/dmdavisauthor
Instagram: www.instagram.com/dmdavisauthor
Twitter: twitter.com/dmdavisauthor
Reader's Group: www.facebook.com/groups/dmdavisreadergroup

Follow me:
BookBub: www.bookbub.com/authors/d-m-davis
Goodreads: www.goodreads.com/dmckdavis

d.m. davis
SEXY WITH HEART
CONTEMPORARY & NEW ADULT ROMANCE AUTHOR

Printed in Great Britain
by Amazon